PUF

Edito

THE GHOSTS

Motley Hall was for sale! And, as the local residents were saying, a good thing too, for it had been looking more derelict every year as it lay empty, gathering layers of dust and ivy and cobwebs, while the owner, the last of the big Uproar family, travelled abroad on his own. Now he was dead (knelt on by an elephant, people said!), and the house would be sold. It didn't matter much, for there was no one left to care – or no one that ordinary people knew about. What they didn't know was that there was a thriving community of GHOSTS at Motley Hall, all of whom were taking a very lively interest in its fate. Motley was much more than a home to them; it was more a rather comfortable prison, because they could never leave it even if they wanted to, so it would be bad luck if it fell into the wrong sort of hands, or worse still, if the house were to be *demolished*. Then they wouldn't stand the *ghost* of a chance.

The future looked frightful, but the ghosts of Motley Hall – Bodkin the clown, Sir Francis the gambler, irascible Sir George the Victorian general, Matt the stable-boy, and the mysterious White Lady – were determined to defend Motley against all comers. And what they lacked in physical force could be made up by powers of a supernatural kind!

This is another excellent comedy, full of funny situations and characters, by the author of *Catweazle* and *Catweazle and the Magic Zodiac*.

For readers of nine and over.

Family Tree of the Uproar Family
(simplified to show succession)

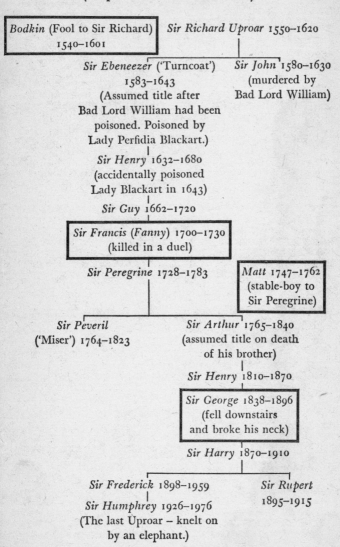

Bodkin (Fool to Sir Richard) 1540–1601

Sir Richard Uproar 1550–1620

Sir Ebeneezer ('Turncoat') 1583–1643
(Assumed title after Bad Lord William had been poisoned. Poisoned by Lady Perfidia Blackart.)

Sir John 1580–1630 (murdered by Bad Lord William)

Sir Henry 1632–1680 (accidentally poisoned Lady Blackart in 1643)

Sir Guy 1662–1720

Sir Francis (Fanny) 1700–1730 (killed in a duel)

Sir Peregrine 1728–1783

Matt 1747–1762 (stable-boy to Sir Peregrine)

Sir Peveril ('Miser') 1764–1823

Sir Arthur 1765–1840 (assumed title on death of his brother)

Sir Henry 1810–1870

Sir George 1838–1896 (fell downstairs and broke his neck)

Sir Harry 1870–1910

Sir Frederick 1898–1959

Sir Rupert 1895–1915

Sir Humphrey 1926–1976 (The last Uproar – knelt on by an elephant.)

Chapter 1

THE wind howled round Motley Hall. It blew the dead leaves along the moss-covered terrace and sent them spinning down the steps to lodge in the long grass of the overgrown lawn. It whistled over the roofs and tossed the rooks against the twisted chimneys; it rippled through the ivy clinging to the walls until the old house seemed to shiver.

For over twenty years Motley Hall had stood empty. From time to time, Mr Arnold Gudgin, a local estate agent, came up from the village to make sure that all the doors and windows were secure and no vandals had broken in.

It had been the home of the Uproar family since the end of the sixteenth century. After the Second World War, Sir Humphrey Uproar, a bachelor who suffered badly from chilblains, had sold most of the furniture and gone off to Thailand. Now, the only inhabitants were ghosts.

The wind continued unabated. Yet inside the house everything was still, almost as if time had been frozen by the cold walls. Grey cobwebs hung everywhere like phantom stalactites. The old billard table, which no one at the auction had wanted, stood shrouded by a dusty sheet, looking in the half-light like an enormous tomb.

Sir George Uproar, Knight Commander of the Most Distinguished Order of St Michael and St George, slowly materialized in the Great Hall. His ghostly form was quivering with indignation and his face, which made one think of a rather conceited old bloodhound, was flushed and puffed with anger. He had found his portrait under an old mangle in the cellars while hunting for some letters, and he was determined to restore it to its proper position over the fireplace.

He remembered how he had stood for hours while 'some German beggar called Winterhalter' had painted it. It showed him standing heroically in his best uniform against a warlike background, where infantry advanced in tidy lines and died in untidy heaps. There were also a few Lancers galloping about and one or two cannon going off, just to balance the composition. He had made sure that Winterhalter painted all his medals a bit bigger and brighter than they actually were, so that they could be easily recognized at a distance.

The cellar door creaked open and, with much puffing and blowing, two more ghosts struggled over to the fireplace with Sir George's picture and dumped it against the panelling.

'Uncommon heavy, ain't it Bodkin?' grumbled the younger of the two, straightening his powdered wig and hitching up a moth-eaten pair of velvet knee-breeches.

Bodkin nodded. 'We'll never get it over the fireplace, Fanny. We ain't Samson and Hercules.'

'Seems silly to bother with it really,' Fanny replied, taking off his wig and using it to dust the frame, 'there's no one in Motley to look at the thing.'

'*I* shall look at it,' growled Sir George.

'What for?' demanded Bodkin. 'You're as dead as a landed herring. Why don't you stop living in the past?'

'That's when I did live, confound you!'

'It's no good getting angry about it. I've been here a lot longer than you –'

'Yes – and got used to it!' snapped Sir George.

Bodkin shook his head sadly, and settled himself against the edge of the billiard table. He had a kindly face, knobbly and lined, with a wry, expressive mouth. As a professional Fool in the days of Elizabeth I he had spent most of his time trying to make people laugh, but there seemed very little to laugh about now. 'I'll let you into a secret,' he told them. 'Sometimes, when I'm feeling low, I go and look at myself in that old cracked glass in the Orangery. "Hello, Bodkin," I whisper, "is that really you?"' He smiled ruefully. 'But all the time I know it ain't, 'cos I can see the wall behind me through my knee-caps.'

There was silence for a while and the three ghosts listened to the melancholy howl of the wind, each of them lost in his own memories.

'The dawn patrols,' murmured Sir George. 'A skirmish in the hills. The thunder of a distant cannonade.' Ghostly tears trickled down his cheeks, and took cover in the grey undergrowth of his moustache.

Bodkin glanced at him worriedly. Something had to be done at once to cheer him up. So, with a wink at Fanny, he pulled a recorder from his belt, hopped on to the stairs and blew the opening notes of a gay Elizabethan jig. 'A little song entitled, "You've got to keep your spirits up or you don't stand the ghost of a chance",' he announced with a flourish.

Sir George ignored him. 'It's got a *haunting* melody,' Bodkin continued. But Sir George went on gazing at his picture.

'Did you hear the story of the banshee who thought that being exorcized meant a twenty-minute walk?' Bodkin asked hopefully.

Sir George stopped feeling sorry for himself and glared at Bodkin.

'I was only trying to cheer you up,' Bodkin explained.

'With puns like that I prefer to be miserable,' snorted Sir George.

There was a howl and the White Lady of Motley Hall materialized on the landing and struck a dramatic pose, mournfully waving her pale draperies. As she came down the stairs she began moaning and sobbing. Bodkin, who was annoyed at being so blatantly upstaged, tried to interrupt her. But she swept up the stairs again, wringing her hands and making the most pitiful cries imaginable. Up and down she went, her pale face streaming with tears.

'White Lady,' said Bodkin. But she ignored him completely. Her howls and groans grew louder, so Bodkin put two fingers in his mouth and whistled with ear-piercing skill. She stopped and glared down at him. Bodkin folded his arms. 'What the Gloriana are you up to?' he asked.

The White Lady answered with great dignity. 'I always do the stairs on Thursday.'

'How do you know it's Thursday?' asked Bodkin innocently.

'It's roughly Thursday,' she airily replied, resuming her restless parade.

'Take no notice,' muttered Sir George, but the moans and cries got even louder.

'Shut up,' yelled Bodkin at the top of his voice.

The White Lady's eyes flashed angrily. 'Don't you

shout at me, you common little clown! If I want to do the stairs, then do the stairs I shall. And if I feel like a good howl I'm perfectly within my rights.'

'Fish-hooks!' retorted Bodkin, who couldn't bear people who overacted.

'You're even vulgarer than usual,' snapped the White Lady.

'You can't say vulgarer,' said Sir George.

'I've just said it,' she retorted. '*Vulgarer!*'

'Couldn't you have a good moan in the Long Gallery?' suggested Fanny.

The White Lady shuddered. 'I loathe the Long Gallery. It gives me the creeps. There's a *something* in there.'

'I know,' said Fanny with a happy smile.

'*You've* sensed it?' breathed the White Lady dramatically.

'I've fed it,' said Fanny. 'It's a mouse.'

The White Lady gave a cry of real fear. 'How horrible!' she gasped.

'No, it isn't. It's very friendly. As a matter of fact I think the little beggar can actually see me. Perhaps he is the seventh son of a seventh son.'

'That wouldn't be hard for mice,' chuckled Bodkin.

'If you must howl, madam,' said Sir George, 'perhaps you could be a little more restrained about it.'

The White Lady looked coldly at them. 'I've lost the urge completely now.'

Bodkin enlisted her help with the problem of getting Sir George's picture up. She and Sir George went to fetch a step-ladder from one of the bedrooms, while Fanny and Bodkin began moving the picture nearer the fireplace. As they heaved it upright, somebody sneezed.

'Bless you,' said Bodkin.

'What for?' said Fanny.

'You sneezed.'

'No, I didn't.'

Bodkin stared at him. 'Are you sure?'

'Of course I am. A fellow knows if he sneezed or not, don't he?'

A second sneeze echoed around the Great Hall. The two ghosts gripped the heavy painting and their voices dropped to a tense whisper. 'Ods bud!' breathed Fanny. 'A trespasser!'

'*One of us?*' queried Bodkin. 'Or one of *them?*'

Fanny hoped it was somebody alive. They were usually less trouble.

'Go and have a look round,' whispered Bodkin.

'Why don't you go?' replied Fanny.

'I'm holding this,' muttered Bodkin.

'So am I,' said Fanny, after thinking about it for a moment.

'Ah! But I'm more scared than you,' said Bodkin quickly.

'Are you?' said Fanny. Bodkin nodded. 'All right,' said Fanny, 'in that case I'll go.' He drew his rapier and crept away into the darkness. A moment later he returned. 'How do you know?' he whispered.

'Know what?' asked Bodkin.

'That you're more scared than me.'

'Well, if I wasn't, I'd be going to look, wouldn't I?' replied Bodkin calmly.

Fanny tried hard to find an answer to this, but it was too difficult for him. He gripped his rapier firmly and once again slunk off to locate the cause of the sneeze.

Had Fanny looked up at the gallery he would have

seen the ghost of a ragged stable-boy who, all this time, had been watching from behind a pillar. Matt – for this was the intruder's name – peered down at Bodkin and stifled another sneeze. Then he concentrated for a moment and vanished from the gallery, to reappear behind Bodkin's back. Quickly, he covered his fingers in soot from the fireplace and drew a pair of spectacles on Sir George's portrait. Then he vanished again, just as the White Lady and Sir George came down the stairs with a step-ladder. 'Where's Fanny?' said Sir George.

'Here,' said Fanny, running back into the Great Hall. He was glad to be back with his friends instead of having to hunt for unknown Sneezes in dark corridors.

The spectacles made him hoot with laughter and the White Lady joined in when she saw them. Bodkin was bewildered. He was holding the picture so he couldn't see what had been done to it. But when Sir George caught sight of Matt's handiwork he became purple with fury. 'Who did that?' he roared.

'Winterhalter,' said Bodkin.

Sir George hurled himself at Bodkin like an avenging angel and grabbed him by his collar. Bodkin let go of the painting and it crashed to the floor. 'You ghastly little vandal!' yelled Sir George, shaking him like a bean-bag.

'What have I done?' choked Bodkin.

'Draw all over me, will you?'

'What are you talking about?'

'Don't play the innocent with me, sir! You've ruined my portrait!'

'I haven't touched your old portrait,' gasped Bodkin.

Sir George relaxed his grip and allowed Bodkin to see the soot spectacles. It was too much for Bodkin and he began to giggle.

'You Elizabethan idiot!' thundered Sir George.

'It wasn't me, I swear it!' said Bodkin trying hard not to laugh. 'The Sneeze – it must have been the Sneeze! Fanny heard it, didn't you, Fanny?'

Without warning the step-ladder collapsed and Sir George got a hearty kick. The White Lady squealed as something pinched her, and a chair skidded across the floor. The ghosts whirled round and round looking for their invisible attacker. 'It's a poltergeist!' shrieked the White Lady.

They heard the sound of feet running up the stairs, a final sneeze, and then silence.

Bodkin was the first to recover. 'That ain't no poltergeist,' he said. 'That is a plain, common-or-garden, now-you-see-it-now-you-don't – *ghost*.'

'Come on, you coward! Show yourself!' boomed Sir George, putting up his fists and dancing round the Great Hall like a prize-fighter.

'He'll appear sooner or later,' said Bodkin philosophically.

'But suppose he don't?' said Sir George. 'And the beggar continues to plague us?'

'I shall have hysterics,' announced the White Lady.

Fanny thought that whatever it was might be frightned. 'Lot of ghosts are,' he said.

'Not of other ghosts,' said Sir George dogmatically.

'Oh yes, they are,' Fanny insisted. 'I remember the first time I saw you after you'd joined us. I was absolutely terrified. You looked so different.'

'Well, he was,' said Bodkin with a grin.

Sir George was determined to track down the intruder and quickly outlined a plan of campaign. Bodkin would have none of it however and told Sir George that he wasn't playing hide-and-seek with a poltergeist and that if they ignored its pranks it would probably go away.

Sir George didn't think much of Bodkin's passive attitude. He had always been a man of action, so he led his search-party up the stairs and ordered them off in different directions to hunt for the mysterious phantom.

As soon as they had gone Matt made himself visible, and crept stealthily down to the Great Hall where Bodkin was once again playing his recorder. As Matt tiptoed behind him, Bodkin heard him and stopped playing. 'And where do you think you're going, Master Sneeze?' he said softly. 'Come here. And no more vanishing tricks!'

Matt swaggered up to Bodkin and struck a defiant attitude which was unfortunately ruined by a sudden sneeze.

'Bless you,' said Bodkin, and boxed the boy's ears.

'That's for the spectacles,' he said. 'And I'll give you another if you get me into any more trouble.'

'See if I care,' said Matt rudely. But he squealed neverthless when Bodkin grabbed him by the ear and pulled him over to the painting. 'Clean it off,' he ordered.

'What's your name?' he asked, as Matt rubbed off the spectacles.

'Matt.'

'Matt, eh? Well, any mat's better for a beating. What sort of mat are you? Door mat? Bath mat? Or prayer mat?'

'I'm Matt, the stable-boy.'

'Then you'd better get back there.'

'I'd a mind to see the house.'

Something was puzzling Bodkin. None of the ghosts could pass outside the house, yet this ragged little spectre had left the stables where he belonged and entered Motley. When he questioned Matt about it the young ghost told him that he was able to roam all over the deserted grounds.

Bodkin asked him how long he had been a ghost, but Matt couldn't remember.

'Who was the King?' Bodkin demanded.

Matt took a George III penny from his pocket. 'It's my lucky penny,' he said.

Bodkin turned it over. It had two heads. 'Very lucky,' he laughed.

'Who are you anyway?' asked Matt.

'I'm Bodkin.'

'That's a funny name.'

'It's meant to be funny. I'm a Fool. You know what a Fool is?'

Matt smiled. 'Yes, the head groom said I was one.'

Bodkin explained patiently. 'A Fool's a clown. A jester. Someone who can sing and dance and play something; do a bit of tumbling, and tell jokes, of course. They wanted a Fool here, see. So as I'd just left the Globe – that's a theatre in London – I got the job. Fool to Sir Richard Uproar. He built this house, as a matter of fact. But the trouble was he had no sense of humour. I just couldn't make him laugh. I tried everything; I used to sit up at night, thinking up really easy jokes. But he never understood any of them. Well, in the end, he got so angry about it, he had me slung in the lily pond. And, would you believe it, he thought that was the funniest thing he'd ever seen! He rolled on the lawn and hooted with laughter until I thought he'd have a fit.

Well, after that, whenever he need cheering up, in I went again. If any special visitors came – splash! Winter or summer, it made no difference. They used to have to break the ice sometimes. Believe me, Matt, it's no joke being funny.'

'Poor old Bodkin,' said Matt sympathetically.

'I caught a permanent cold,' said Bodkin. 'It finished me in the end.'

'It was a cold finished me,' said Matt. 'The stables were damp and the wind was like a knife in the winter.'

He began asking about the other ghosts and Bodkin told him as much as he knew. How Sir George had filled himself with brandy one night, fallen down the stairs and broken his neck. How Fanny had gambled away the family fortune, and fought dozens of duels. 'A real rake he was,' said Bodkin. 'You know what a rake is, don't you?'

'Yes,' said Matt. 'A long wooden thing.'

Bodkin laughed loudly. 'That's Fanny all right!'

'What about her in white?' asked Matt.

'Well, we don't know *who* she is. And she says she doesn't know either. But I'm not so sure. Trouble is, I don't remember when she first began haunting, or even who she was before that. One thing's certain, she never stops moaning.'

'You're all company for each other though, aren't you?' said Matt a trifle wistfully, remembering his long years of being alone.

'I suppose so,' said Bodkin. 'But they've heard my jokes hundreds of times.' He jumped to his feet. 'Here – do you know the one about –'

'I'd best be getting back –'

Bodkin sighed. 'All right,' he said, 'some other time.

Matt frowned with the effort he needed to vanish, and faded until he was only a faint mist. Then he said, 'Are you going to tell 'em it was me?'

Bodkin shook his head. 'Of course not. But there's one thing I want to know.'

'What's that?' said Matt.

'You said you'd never been here before. So what made you come today – eh?'

Matt's misty form became solid again. 'I wanted to look at the house before they pulled it down,' he said.

'What did you say?'

Matt looked puzzled. Surely Bodkin and the other ghosts knew about it?

'I said, I wanted to see inside Motley Hall before it was pulled down,' he repeated.

Chapter 2

'I DON'T believe it,' said Sir George. 'The boy's lying.'

The search for the Sneeze had been abandoned when Bodkin frantically summoned the ghosts back to the Great Hall. Now they stood facing their young visitor and listening to his terrible news.

'It's quite absurd,' said the White Lady, 'Sir Humphrey would never allow it.'

'Sir Humphrey ain't got no choice in the matter,' said Bodkin. 'He's . . .'

'Humphrey? Gone to earth?' gasped Sir George.

Bodkin nodded gravely. 'You'd better listen to what Matt's got to tell us,' he said.

Matt had been in the stables the previous day when two men had sheltered from a heavy downpour. There was something furtive about them, so he had listened to their whispered conversation. He'd learnt that Sir Humphrey, the last of the Uproars, had been knelt on by an elephant in Thailand. The two men had discussed his death and the future of Motley Hall, and had agreed that now the owner was dead the house was certain to be put on the market. One of them, a fat and greedy-looking man called Brayling, had promised to pay the other, a Mr Penrose, several thousand pounds to write a report proving Motley Hall was no longer safe and recommending that it should be demolished.

'And if I say Motley's to come down,' Penrose had whispered, 'nothing on earth can save it'!

There was silence in the Great Hall when Matt finished telling his story to the ghosts. For a while they were all too stunned to say anything. Then the White Lady began crying.

'Woe to Motley Hall! Doom is on the House of Uproar. All is lost, lost!'

'I wish you were!' murmured Bodkin under his breath.

'But was that all?' Fanny asked. 'Didn't they say anything else?'

'No,' said Matt, 'that were the end of it.'

'The end of us, more like,' muttered Bodkin. 'Stuck out in the open, that's what we'll be.'

'We must stop them,' declared Sir George, standing stiff as a ramrod. 'This is our home!'

But it seemed an impossible task for mere phantoms, and the White Lady drifted dejectedly towards the Bell Tower. 'I'd better toll the bell,' she said sadly. 'I always ring it when there's been a death in the family.'

'I'm a great believer in tradition, Madam,' said Sir George, 'but this is hardly the time for campanology.'

'Or bell-ringing,' said Fanny.

The White Lady explained that the local people expected it. She pointed out that it was mentioned in the guide books, and then melted mournfully away.

'Couldn't you scare villains off?' asked Matt.

Sir George gave Matt a look of withering scorn. 'Haven't you learned anything since you passed on?' he said. 'We can't make people see us, surely you know that. Either they can or they can't. It's not up to us!'

This was true. The ghosts couldn't appear to human beings at will. It was, as Sir George had once tried to explain to Fanny, a question of wave-lengths. A mournful booming echoed throughout Motley Hall as the White Lady swung despairingly to and fro on the end of the bell-rope.

'To think there's been an Uproar in Motley since the seventeenth century!' exclaimed Sir George unhappily.

'And it's still going on!' shouted Bodkin, above the noise.

'I say,' yelled Fanny. 'Can you hear a motor car?'

'Only just!' Bodkin yelled back. He sent Matt to tell the White Lady they had had enough of the bell, and joined Fanny and Sir George at the grime-covered windows.

'It's so light out there,' muttered Sir George, 'I can't see a thing.'

A key turned squeakily in the iron-studded door and the bolts were slid back. Mr Gudgin, a little mouse of a man, tiptoed in just as the bell stopped tolling.

'It's stopped,' he said to his companion. 'It always tolls after a death in the family, Mr Penrose.'

The ghosts exchanged glances, remembering that Mr Penrose was one of the villains Matt had told them about.

'Do you mean the place is haunted?' said Penrose.

'Well, the villagers say it is,' said Gudgin. Then he gasped when he saw Sir George's painting. 'I thought I'd put that in the cellar!'

'You had,' muttered Sir George, 'but I got it out again.'

The only ghost Gudgin had ever seen was the White Lady, who had appeared to him as a white blur at the end of a corridor, during one of his routine inspections of the house. But he knew there were many stories about ghosts in Motley Hall so he was nervous every time he came.

'That's Sir George Uproar,' he said, indicating the picture. 'General Uproar he was.'

'Still is,' said Fanny bowing politely to Sir George.

'He looks a bit dim,' said Penrose.

'Insufferable bounder!' roared Sir George.

'He was known as "Crocodile Uproar" you know,' Gudgin explained. 'You see, once when he was campaigning in Egypt he had to cross the Nile to attack the enemy. Unfortunately, there was no time to build a bridge so he ordered his regiment to swim across.'

Sir George began to look uncomfortable.

'When he was told that that part of the river was infested with crocodiles,' Gudgin went on, 'Sir George replied that one British soldier was worth ten crocodiles.' He paused significantly. 'As it turned out, one crocodile was worth ten British soldiers. However, he continued to advance with a somewhat depleted force and joined the other regiments for the Battle of El Khasi. Unfortunately, because of the smoke and confusion, he attacked the wrong way, and when it was all over he discovered he'd captured most of Her Majesty's Eighth Hussars.'

Sir George was spluttering with embarrassment while Bodkin and Fanny merely grinned at his discomfiture.

'It was a wonderful family, you know, Mr Penrose,' said Gudgin. 'Part of the fabric of English history. But all things come to an end, and now the Uproars are no more and the dear old place must be sold.'

Penrose glanced impatiently at his watch and asked if anyone was thinking of buying Motley. Gudgin told him that there had been a tentative inquiry from an American who wanted to ship the house stone by stone to the United States, and rebuild it in the middle of Las Vegas.

'Where's Las Vegas?' asked Fanny.

'I've no idea,' grunted Sir George. 'But it sounds damn foreign to me.'

Just then Matt and the White Lady reappeared and the boy pointed excitedly at Penrose.

'That's one of 'em!' he said.

'We know,' said Bodkin.

Penrose looked at his watch again. 'I don't want to alarm you, Mr Gudgin, but I think I ought to warn you that the whole place may prove to be unsafe.'

'Surprise, surprise!' murmured the White Lady cynically.

'Not safe?' exclaimed Gudgin. 'What makes you say that?'

'Money,' said Bodkin.

Penrose smiled. 'Now don't get worried, Mr Gudgin. I'm just warning you, that's all. Don't forget, Motley has been empty for twenty years. It's probably running with damp and full of woodworm, dry rot, and heaven knows what else.'

'Us,' volunteered Fanny.

Gudgin protested that Motley was perfectly sound. He had looked after the house most conscientiously and it was in an excellent state of preservation.

'That's for me to decide,' said Penrose. 'In my official capacity,' he added pointedly. 'Now if you don't mind –' And once more he looked at his watch.

'He's trying to get rid of him,' muttered Sir George.

'Maybe the other man's coming,' suggested the White Lady.

'That's it,' said Bodkin. 'He's probably bringing Penrose's money!'

Matt ran out to see if Brayling was lurking in the stables. The other ghosts looked longingly at the open door and the tantalizing view of the park. If only they could get out as easily as Matt!

Meanwhile, Penrose began busying himself with various pieces of measuring equipment. He had gauges to measure any movement of the walls or floors and these he now placed in various parts of the Great Hall.

Gudgin watched him, now very worried over his gloomy forecast. 'If you could drop the keys in at my office when you've finished,' he said, 'I'd be most grateful.'

'I won't forget,' murmured Penrose, getting a spirit-level from his bag.

But the moment Gudgin left, Penrose stopped pretending to work, and sat down to read his paper. It was clear to the ghosts that he was waiting for Brayling to turn up.

'The man's a rotter!' muttered Sir George.

'Such a nasty cruel face,' said the White Lady.

'And we are powerless to stop him! Mere onlookers!'

'We need a plan!' said Fanny.

'I'm trying to think of one!' Bodkin muttered.

'So am I,' said Fanny. 'But my mind's a blank!'

It usually is, thought Bodkin. 'Whatever happens,' he declared, 'we won't give up Motley without a fight!'

'That's the spirit!' said Sir George, quite unaware of the awful pun he'd made.

Matt came running in. 'Brayling's on his way,' he told them excitedly.

A large red-faced man strolled in carrying a small

case which he dumped ostentatiously on the billiard table. 'So that was your Mr Gudgin, was it?' he said to Penrose. 'He's not going to make any trouble for us, is he?'

Penrose folded his paper. 'He'll try, Mr Brayling, he'll try.'

Bodkin was quite sure that the case held the money for Penrose, and he waited patiently until the two men turned from the billiard table. Then, quickly, he took the thick bundles of paper money from the case. He knew that the sight of the case apparently opening by itself would have ruined his plan.

Penrose's mackintosh lay across a tea-chest, so, with a wink at his friends, Bodkin arranged the money beneath it, just as the two men walked back to the billard table.

'Would you like to count it?' said Brayling.

The ghosts waited eagerly as Penrose opened the case, while Brayling looked discreetly out of the window.

'Are you being funny?' said Penrose, looking up from the empty case.

'What do you mean?' said Brayling.

'This case is empty!'

'That was very quick of you, Penrose,' said Brayling with a knowing chuckle.

'Don't play games with me!' snapped Penrose.

'You're the one who's playing games. Where have you put it?'

The two men were soon shouting at each other. Penrose accused Brayling of failing to bring his money, and Brayling accused Penrose of hiding it. At the height of their quarrel Bodkin tweaked Penrose's coat so that it fell off the tea-chest and the bundles of notes were revealed.

'My case was empty, was it?' snarled Brayling. 'I knew you were a tricky customer, Penrose, but I didn't think you'd try something like this!'

'Brayling, I swear –'

'The deal's off,' said Brayling. 'I can't do business with such naïve dishonesty. I've plenty of other contacts. I'll get rid of Motley Hall without help from your department!' He was getting his money back when he suddenly saw Mr Gudgin standing in the doorway.

Gudgin had come back to question Penrose about the future of Motley Hall. Instead he had overheard the quarrel and realized what Penrose had been up to.

'I've seen and heard quite enough,' he said coldly. 'I think you'd both better leave at once before I take this matter further.'

That night the ghosts sat round the billiard table well pleased with themselves. They had achieved something at last. Sir George pointed out that if Matt hadn't warned them of the impending danger they might not have realized it until Motley Hall was tumbling round their ghostly ears, and all of them agreed that Matt was to have 'the freedom of Motley Hall' to come and go as he pleased.

The ghosts knew that there were likely to be many battles ahead, if they were to keep Motley safe, but they had something to strive for, and a common purpose.

'And now,' said Sir George, pointing at his portrait, 'let's hang that over the fireplace!'

Chapter 3

'Now that the house is for sale,' boomed Sir George, 'we face the possibility of *people*.' He had called a meeting to discuss the situation. He liked meetings. They gave him an opportunity to exert his authority, and he felt the other ghosts gained much from his leadership.

Bodkin stood up. 'Well, I'm glad Motley is for sale. I like people in the place. It gives us something to talk about and it's fun if any of them can see us.'

'Fun! I find it very off-putting,' retorted Sir George. 'The beggars stare so.'

'I agree,' the White Lady rejoined. 'It's most embarrassing.'

'Fish-hooks!' muttered Bodkin. 'You *try* to be seen! What about John Longstaff – eh, Fanny?'

Fanny, who had been idly watching a moth flying round the Great Hall, said, 'John who?'

'John Longstaff,' repeated Bodkin patiently. 'You remember him. 1920s. A thin lad with a banjo. And spots.'

'I remember the banjo,' said Fanny.

Bodkin nudged the White Lady. 'You followed him everywhere, didn't you? Even into the bathroom.'

'*I did not!*' said the White Lady, banging the billiard table in her anger and making a cloud of dust rise in the air.

'The poor lad passed out when he saw her,' Bodkin went on remorselessly. 'In fact he'd have drowned if I hadn't pulled the plug out!'

'*I* pulled the plug out!' said the White Lady vehemently.

Bodkin laughed with gleeful triumph, and she was so angry at the way he had tricked her, she vanished without another word.

'I'm sorry,' said Bodkin. 'Come back. I didn't mean it!'

Slowly the White Lady became visible again. She glared at Bodkin and then pointedly turned her back on him.

Sir George tried to return to the main reason for the meeting. 'What do you think?' he asked Fanny.

'Someone pulled the plug out,' said Fanny, still thinking about John Longstaff.

'*About people living in Motley!*' roared Sir George.

'Oh yes,' said Fanny, pulling himself together. 'Well, I agree with Bodkin. It's uncommon dull without 'em.'

'That's all very well,' said Sir George. 'But I can't bear being walked through.'

'Well nobody *likes* it,' agreed Fanny.

Matt hadn't said much, because he was a newcomer, but now he put up his hand to attract Sir George's attention.

'It depends who buys the place, don't it?' he argued. 'They could be all right! but if they weren't we could put them off, couldn't we?'

The ghosts thought about this for a moment. It was an appealing idea and Sir George's eyes flashed with the light of battle. He reached for his notebook. 'Has anyone any suggestions?' he asked.

The White Lady's idea was first. 'We could write something on the wall. Something quite nice,' she added hastily. 'But at the same time *firm*. A poem perhaps, with a touch of melancholy.'

Bodkin stood up.

> 'We are the ghosts of Motley,
>   We're British through and through –'

he declaimed.

> 'But please don't come and live here –'

Fanny added.

> 'Or we'll make a ghost of you,'

finished Bodkin.

Sir George and the White Lady looked coldly at them, while Bodkin grinned back, and Fanny and Matt sniggered.

'How about: "Trespassers will be haunted"?' Bodkin suggested.

'Must you always play the fool?' bellowed Sir George.

'But I *am* a Fool,' said Bodkin. 'It's my job.'

Sir George was still thinking of a cutting reply, when the ghosts heard the main door being unlocked. Without another word they all vanished into the shadows on the landing. It was Mr Gudgin again. With him was Mr Wallace, who worked for the British Banana Company. Mr Gudgin was hoping that the British Banana Company would buy Motley Hall.

'Sir Humphrey lived abroad,' he explained, as Wallace looked round the Great Hall. 'He owned a rubber plantation. He died out there. He was knelt on.'

'Knelt on?' said Mr Wallace.

'By an elephant. They say it was very quick.'

'The elephant?'

'No – the accident,' said Mr Gudgin.

Wallace listened impatiently while he was told what a

bargain the British Banana Company would be getting. 'All this panelling is Elizabethan,' Gudgin explained. 'Linen-fold they call it.' And he ran his hand gently over the carved oak.

'It will have to come out,' said Wallace, who preferred cork tiles. 'We'll gut the interior of course. By the time we've finished, you won't know the place.'

Gudgin was shocked, and so were the ghosts.

'You think I'm a vandal, don't you, Mr Gudgin?' said Wallace with a grin. 'But there's dozens of these old places. And they're all falling to bits because nobody wants them. This one at least would be saved.'

'I suppose so,' murmured Gudgin. 'But it wouldn't look the same, would it?'

But Wallace paid little attention to him. He was examining the staircase. 'This is splendid!' he exclaimed.

'Jacobean,' said Gudgin proudly.

'I don't care if it's Anglo-Saxon,' said Wallace cheerfully, 'it's just the place for the lifts.'

Although the ghosts didn't know what lifts were the White Lady looked even paler than usual when she realized that Wallace was going to rip out her beloved staircase. She watched glumly with the others as he banged at the panelling to check there was no woodworm.

Suddenly a small section of it slid back. Wallace recovered quickly from his surprise and peered into the hole.

Bodkin became strangely agitated. 'Leave it alone! Don't touch it!' he warned. But Wallace couldn't see or hear him, and reached cautiously into the opening and brought out a silver sword hilt.

Gudgin looked at it in amazement, and shivered as a

sudden gust of wind howled through the Great Hall and whistled away down the gloomy corridor.

'Put it back!' cried Bodkin desperately.

Wallace held the sword hilt up to the light. 'This ought to fetch something,' he breathed.

'It'll fetch something all right!' muttered Bodkin.

Wallace put the sword hilt in his case.

'Surely it belongs to the house,' said Gudgin feebly.

'Who's to know that?' said Wallace. 'We can split anything we get for it. Nobody knew it was there, so who's to know where we got it from? Besides' – Wallace gave Gudgin a nudge – 'you do want to sell this place, don't you?' Gudgin nodded feebly. 'Right,' said Wallace, picking up his case, 'let's have a look at the Long Gallery.'

As the two of them left the Great Hall, the panel slid shut.

'We've got to get that sword hilt back,' said Bodkin. He told the others how Sir John Uproar had fallen foul of Lord William Firkin, or 'Bad' Lord William as he was called. Sir John had found out just how bad he was when Lord William pushed him off Beachy Head. It had been a fatal revelation. Bad Lord William next tried to murder Ebenezer Uproar, Sir John's younger brother. But Ebenezer escaped to Ireland, thus enabling Lord William to take over Motley Hall.

Bad Lord William had owned the largest private collection of thumbscrews in the land. He built his own gallows on the roof and arranged executions for his friends to watch – usually acting as hangman himself. His reign of terror finally ended when the cook put hemlock in his soup. Even then Bad Lord William hadn't finished with Motley. He began haunting the house, looking everywhere for his sword. When he found it, he would float about, waving it at anyone who crossed his path. Eventually the sword was deliberately broken by Ebenezer, who had come back from Ireland, and the hilt was put into the secret chamber. As long as the sword hilt was locked away, Lord William's spirit was powerless. 'But now it's been taken out, he'll be up to all his old tricks again,' concluded Bodkin. 'And he won't be in a very good mood after three hundred years!'

'But he can't haunt us!' exclaimed Fanny.

'He can haunt anyone!' said Bodkin gloomily.

The ghostly wind rushed back into the Great Hall and howled round the billiard table like a banshee. Then it rushed to the library door and threw it open. There, on the threshold, stood Bad Lord William dressed in black from top to toe. The howling wind died away as he came menacingly towards Sir George. 'Who are you, you old goat?' he snarled.

Sir George stood his ground defiantly. 'Uproar's my name, sir,' he said. 'General Sir George Uproar, K.C.M.G. And I'd trouble you to –'

'You'll not trouble me a jot,' interrupted Bad Lord William, turning abruptly to face Bodkin. 'Your name, custard-face?'

'B – B – B – Bodkin.'

Bad Lord William sneered and held a ghostly dagger under Bodkin's chin. 'I also have a bodkin. 'Tis exceeding sharp. How sharp are you?'

'Not sharp, my lord,' said Bodkin trembling. 'I'm blunt.'

Bad Lord William began to enjoy himself. 'To be blunt is to be to the point. How say you – a blunt *and* pointed bodkin? Such a thing is impossible.' He gave Bodkin a little dig in the belly.

'Ow!' said Bodkin. 'I'm not very good at puns.'

Fanny rushed forward impetuously. 'Let him be, you great bully!' he cried.

'I'll have you flogged raw!' hissed Bad Lord William, who expected everyone to be afraid of him. 'I am master here!'

'Of course you are,' cooed the White Lady, doing her best to calm him down. 'It must have been a terrible strain for you, locked up in the woodwork all these years; you need time to get used to things, and make yourself at home.'

'*I am at home!*' roared Bad Lord William, making them all tremble. 'Who lives here now?' he demanded.

'Nobody,' said Matt.

'Scullion! I saw two of them!'

'But they don't *live* here!' said Matt.

Bodkin seized his chance. 'But if they have their way, Lord William,' he said, 'hundreds of people will be coming – and they'll change everything. You won't know the place. It'll be noisy – and brightly lit. You won't like it, my lord. You'd be far better off somewhere else. Wouldn't he?' finished Bodkin, appealing to the others.

Bad Lord William narrowed his cruel eyes and gave them a wolfish grin. 'If they have their way – eh? Then they shall not have their way. They shall be silenced! Silenced for ever!'

Chapter 4

'WE'LL start with the cellars this afternoon,' said Wallace, as he and Gudgin left Motley Hall to have lunch in the village.

This gave Bad Lord William another of his nasty ideas. 'I shall entomb them in the cellars! They are doomed!' With this chilling thought, he vanished, as the ghostly wind which always seemed to accompany him once again howled through Motley.

'He must have had a very unhappy childhood,' said the White Lady in the silence that followed his going.

Matt said that they'd never get rid of Bad Lord William until the sword hilt was back inside the panel.

Fanny was angry with Sir George. 'You wanted to keep the house empty. Well, it looks as if Bad Lord William's going to do it for you.'

'I draw the line at killing people,' retorted Sir George uncomfortably.

'Oh?' said Bodkin, 'I thought you were a General.'

'We mustn't quarrel,' said Matt quickly. 'We've got to stick together.'

'The boy's right,' muttered Sir George, glowering at Bodkin. 'We must meet this challenge absolutely united.'

'That's it!' the White Lady said to Fanny. 'A *challenge!* A duel! You must challenge him, and if you win he'll be banished to the attics. After all, we never go up there.'

Fanny thought the duel was a splendid notion and got very excited about it. Then he went rather quiet and told his friends there was something they had overlooked.

'It's such a tiny thing, I hardly like to mention it,' he said.

'What is it?' asked Sir George.

'What if I lose?'

Everyone made reassuring noises and patted him on the back. 'You can't possibly lose,' said Sir George firmly.

But Bodkin was worried about something else. 'Even if Fanny beats Lord William,' he said, 'we've still got to stop the British Banana Company.'

'The defeat of Lord William is the first objective,' said Sir George. 'We can decide the rest of the campaign later.'

Matt delivered the challenge to Lord William who was surprised to meet such strong resistance. However, he felt sure he would have no trouble beating Fanny, and arranged to fight him in the Long Gallery.

Unfortunately Fanny found a bottle of Sir George's best Napoleon brandy, which he swigged to give himself courage: Matt found him staggering about, fighting drunk and quite sure he would quickly finish off Bad Lord William. Matt was dismayed to see him in such a state, but Fanny told him that he fought better when he was drunk. Then he took another swig from the bottle and burst into song. 'For youth's a flower that soon doth fade,' he burbled. 'And life is but a span.' With this happy thought the tipsy phantom slid to the floor, grinning foolishly, as the other ghosts appeared around him.

'He can't fight Lord William!' said Matt.

'He can't fight a gooseberry bush,' groaned Bodkin.

Fanny looked hazily at them. 'Oh yes I can. I can fight any gooseberry bush growing,' he mumbled, and started to sing again.

'I hope you like it in the attics,' said Bodkin grimly, grabbing the bottle from him.

'He's finished it!' said Sir George furiously.

'He's finished the lot of us!' said Bodkin. 'And Wallace and Gudgin as well.'

Then Lord William appeared, with his sword drawn and a murderous gleam in his eye. He took one look at Fanny and began to laugh. 'The noodle's drunk!' he said scornfully.

Fanny staggered to his feet and valiantly tried to raise his sword. Then he swayed gently to and fro and slowly keeled over backwards and crashed to the floor with an owlish expression on his face.

'To the attics with him!' ordered Lord William.

'That's not fair!' said Matt.

It was lucky for all of them that Lord William suddenly heard Gudgin and Wallace arriving back from the village. Sheathing his sword he ran down to the Great Hall and followed the two men into the cellars.

Something had to be done to stop him carrying out his threat, and the ghosts were still arguing about the best course of action to take, when Bodkin grabbed Fanny's sword and ran after Lord William.

Bodkin found him just as the wicked lord was about to bolt Gudgin and Wallace in the cellar.

At first he laughed to see Bodkin with a sword in his hand, but when Bodkin attacked him, his laughter stopped and the fight was on. Up and down the Great Hall they went, cutting and thrusting at each other. Bodkin's fencing experience had been limited to a couple of stage fights at the Globe Theatre, but he was very quick on his feet and whenever Lord William's blade looked particularly dangerous, he vanished into thin air, and then reappeared at a safer distance. This startling ploy annoyed Lord William, especially whenever he was about to deliver the *coup de grâce*. With a roar, he chased Bodkin round the billiard table, while Sir George and the others watched fearfully. The fury of Lord William's next attack nearly brought Bodkin to his knees, and the two of them struggled together, hilt to hilt.

'What's the difference between a hanged man and a beheaded man?' gasped Bodkin, desperately playing for time.

'What *is* the difference between a hanged man and a beheaded man?' asked Lord William.

'There's no difference,' Bodkin replied. 'They both get it in the neck.' Then he pushed Lord William away and took refuge on the opposite side of the billiard table.

'Scullion! Varlet! Poltroon!' screamed Lord William.

'It's no good calling me names,' said Bodkin, 'I'm puffed.'

Lord William leapt across the billiard table like a tiger and again Bodkin was forced to retreat.

'Get those two fools out of the cellar!' yelled Bodkin to Sir George, but, although Lord William hadn't managed to bolt the cellar door, it had jammed shut, and try as they might, Gudgin and Wallace couldn't push it open. It wasn't long before Gudgin began to panic and shout for help. Wallace told him dourly to save his breath. 'Nobody can hear you,' he said.

'Oh, but we can!' said the White Lady, who had just reached the other side of the door with Matt and Sir George. 'If only they knew we were here!'

'I don't think they would want to,' muttered Sir George, tugging ineffectually at the door handle. 'If we had something to lever it with, we might get it open.'

This gave Matt an idea. He raced back to the Great Hall, where Bodkin was still fighting off Lord William, and ran to get the sword hilt from Wallace's case. Bad Lord William lunged at him but Matt ducked under the blade and rushed back down the cellar steps. Using the sword hilt the ghosts slowly levered the door open, much to the astonishment of Gudgin and Wallace, who could see nothing except the sword hilt floating in the air! Then Matt and the others ran back with it to the Great Hall and searched feverishly for the secret panel. They banged away at the woodwork to no avail, while Bad Lord William tried to get at them, but Bodkin attacked him fiercely and kept him at bay. Finally Bad Lord William lunged at Bodkin so savagely that his sword splintered the panelling.

It was the place the ghosts had been looking for! The panel slid back to reveal the secret hiding place. Swiftly, Matt popped in the sword hilt and slammed the panel shut. There was a howl from Bad Lord William, and he melted away as mysteriously as he had appeared.

Bodkin collapsed on a tea-chest, exhausted, while the rest of the ghosts gathered round to congratulate him.

'You were so brave,' said the White Lady. 'I didn't think you had it in you!'

'I nearly had it in me several times!' panted Bodkin.

'Somehow I think we've seen the last of Mr Wallace,' Sir George remarked as the two men ran up from the cellar and made frantically for the door.

'I'll drink to that,' said Fanny.

'Not if I can help it,' said Bodkin.

Chapter 5

THE Bell Tower was a favourite meeting place for the ghostly residents of Motley Hall. Every Tuesday they played a noisy quarrelsome game of bridge there and held acrimonious post mortems after every rubber. Bodkin and Sir George played against Fanny and the White Lady. Bodkin hated bridge and didn't really understand it, but because it was a four-handed game the others couldn't play without him. He preferred a racy Elizabethan card game called Gleek, but because Gleek was for three people, he never got the chance to play it. He was remembering how he, and Will Shakespeare, and another actor called Burbage used to play Gleek in the tiring-house at the Globe theatre, when Sir George suddenly shouted at him: 'You trumped my ace! I'll have you shot at dawn!'

'Couldn't you make it sunset?' Bodkin retorted swiftly. 'I hate getting up early!'

Fanny, who was surprisingly good at cards, totted up the score. 'That's twenty-three thousand, five hundred and thirty pounds they owe us,' he told the White Lady.

'Are you sure?' gasped Sir George.

Fanny nodded.

'And what do they owe us?' Sir George asked Bodkin.

'Fifty-one pounds and ten shillings,' said Bodkin sheepishly.

'I think we should change partners for the next hundred years,' Sir George said. 'This half-baked theatrical ham hasn't the foggiest idea how to play.'

'I'm good at Triumph,' said Bodkin indignantly.

'How many times do I have to tell you it's not called Triumph any more,' said Sir George testily. 'It's called whist.'

'It was Triumph in Elizabeth's day.'

'And it was whist by Victoria's,' said Sir George. 'And, I believe, still is.'

Sir George had taught them bridge and he felt humiliated that the White Lady and Fanny always won so easily.

'When do you have to pay 'em?' asked Matt, who had been watching the game without understanding it at all.

'When we find the treasure,' Sir George answered.

He explained that an ancestor of his, Sir Peveril Uproar, had been a miser who amassed a fortune and then spent the rest of his life counting it. There were rumours that 'Sir Peveril's hoard' was still hidden in the house. Sir George had searched everywhere for it during his lifetime without success.

However, there was a more recent mystery at Motley Hall. Several days before, eight large cardboard boxes had been dumped behind the staircase. None of the ghosts knew who had put them there, but the boxes had Japanese writing on them and things like 'This Side Up' and 'Fragile'. Bodkin and Fanny had carried one up to the Bell Tower and now it was being used as a bridge table.

'Is there anything inside it?' Matt asked curiously.

'A wireless,' said Bodkin, shuffling the cards.

'What's a wireless?' asked Matt. He had been in the stables for two hundred years and hadn't seen much of the twentieth century except for the occasional car or aeroplane.

Fanny patted the cardboard box. 'I don't think these are wirelesses,' he said. 'They've got glass fronts.'

'They've got knobs on,' said Bodkin, beginning to deal.

'So's a chest of drawers,' Fanny retorted.

The argument grew heated, till eventually Bodkin bet Fanny ten guineas that the box contained a wireless set. Then he swept the cards from the top, opened it up, and took out a small portable television set. Sir Humphrey Uproar hadn't had television, so the ghosts had never seen one before. Bodkin pointed to the switches. 'On. Off. Volume.' He held out his hand. 'It's a wireless. Ten guineas, Fanny!'

'Tatyama,' read Fanny. 'It's not a wireless – it's a tatyama. Whatever that is.'

Sir George backed away from it. 'It sounds jolly foreign to me. I'd leave it alone if I were you. It might go off.'

'Fish-hooks!' muttered Bodkin, and turned it on. The set flickered for a moment and then a picture appeared. 'Gloriana!' breathed Bodkin, hardly able to believe his eyes.

'No. Tatyama!' said Fanny, absolutely fascinated.

'Great Caesar's ghost!' gasped Sir George. Fanny looked round nervously.

'Where!' he said.

A dozen horses were galloping along accompanied by the disembodied voice of a race commentator. The ghosts watched the race with awe, mesmerized by the amazing invention. As the horses thundered towards the winning-post they began urging them on excitedly.

Meanwhile in the Great Hall, two young criminals

were looking at the television sets they had stolen and wondering why one of them was missing. 'It's been stolen, Jeffrey,' said Ronald indignantly.

'Do you think some kids have taken it?' said Jeffrey. 'What a dirty trick.'

'Kids wouldn't come here. In fact no one local would, 'cos this place is supposed to be haunted. That's why I chose it. Let's have a look round. Whoever's taken it might still be here.'

In the Bell Tower the ghosts – Sir George, Fanny and the White Lady – continued to watch the race-meeting avidly.

'Are they going to sit in front of that thing all day?' Matt asked Bodkin.

'All day and every day,' murmured Bodkin gloomily. 'It can't go on for ever, can it?'

'Of course not,' said Bodkin. 'It'll run out of horses.'

Matt reminded him there were seven more Tatyamas in the Great Hall. Bodkin looked at the others sitting with their chins cupped in their hands, staring at the screen, and then deliberately blocked their view. They complained noisily, but he stayed where he was.

'What's got into you?' he asked them angrily. 'Staring at this blessed box of tricks with your eyes popping out of your heads like a crowd at an execution. This thing's a blooming Gorgon if you ask me, and if it don't drive you mad it'll turn you to stone!'

Sir George tried to push him out of the way. 'You superstitious blockhead!'

Bodkin switched off and the screen went blank, amid howls of protest. 'Bring back the horses, you rogue!' Fanny yelled, and reached for his sword.

'Turn it on!' screamed the White Lady.

'Fish-hooks!' said Bodkin calmly, and Matt and he vanished from the Bell Tower.

'By heavens, we shall watch it!' roared Sir George fumbling with the switches. He managed to turn the set on again, but unwittingly he changed to another channel and also increased the volume. The smiling face of a cookery demonstrator appeared. 'Hello,' she said at the top of her voice.

'Don't shout at me, ma'am! I ain't deaf!' said Sir George savagely.

The White Lady leant forward and adjusted the volume. 'What's happened to the racing?' she asked irritably.

A large ornamental cake suddenly came on the screen. It appeared to shrink as the demonstrator walked up to it. 'As you see,' she said, 'this is the perfect cake for your children's party.'

'Stand aside!' bellowed Sir George. 'You're blocking my view of the horses!'

'Have you pencil and paper handy?' inquired the cookery demonstrator, completely ignoring Sir George.

'No,' said Fanny.

'Good,' she smiled. 'Then I'll begin –'

'Get out of the way, you pale-faced trollop!' snarled Sir George.

The White Lady tugged at his Norfolk jacket. 'I'd quite like to know how to make Angel Cake,' she said quietly. 'It might be useful if I ever . . . "move on". '

But Sir George didn't want to learn cake-making. He wanted to watch the three o'clock race at Newmarket. Beside himself with rage, he picked up the set and shook it furiously. Then he remembered that there were seven more of the magical contraptions sitting in the Great Hall so he banged it down on its box. 'I'll get one for myself,' he muttered savagely.

When Sir George had gone, the White Lady and Fanny sank back into a glassy-eyed stupor. They were completely under the spell of television.

After the cookery demonstration, an Indian Professor began talking about yoga. It wasn't a subject any of the phantoms knew much about.

'I'm going to ask each of you a very personal question,' he said with a smile. 'When was the last time you breathed? *Really* breathed?'

Fanny and the White Lady looked at each other. It was a difficult question to answer.

The Professor smiled again. 'Well, we're going to change all that,' he said confidently.

'I don't think you are,' said Fanny sadly.

Bodkin decided to hide the rest of the magic boxes in Motley Hall's secret passage. This had been built during the Civil War to provide an escape route for the Uproar family if Cromwell's troops ever attacked the house. It was opened by turning a carved gryphon on the newel post at the bottom of the stairs. But before Matt and he could put the plan into action they heard footsteps approaching. Quickly Bodkin closed the entrance. Then the two ghosts hid in the shadows. There was always a possibility they might be seen by someone sensitive to their presence.

A policeman tiptoed into the Great Hall, sucking a cut finger.

'What's he?' whispered Matt. 'A soldier?'

Bodkin shook his head. 'He's a policeman.'

'What do they do?'

'Well, they sit in the kitchen and eat jam tarts; drink tea, and tickle the cook; and find stolen bicycles.'

Bodkin's knowledge of the police was based on what he'd seen in Motley Hall and therefore somewhat sketchy.

'And what's –' Matt began.

'A two-wheeled mechanical horse,' said Bodkin, anticipating his question.

The policeman found the stolen television sets. 'Hello – hello!' he said.

Matt was puzzled. 'Is he talking to us?'

'No – they always say that,' muttered Bodkin.

'He looks pleased,' said Matt. 'Do you think he wants one?'

'He can have 'em all as far as I'm concerned,' said Bodkin.

The policeman knew that eight sets had been stolen. Was the other one still in the house? He moved off quietly to investigate.

As soon as he had gone Bodkin and Matt hid the seven boxes in the secret passage. 'That's put paid to their silly gazing,' said Bodkin with satisfaction.

They had just closed the entrance when Sir George appeared. He was very chagrined to find the boxes gone, and after a moment's angry indecision he marched moodily off into the library.

Jeffrey and Ronald were just as upset when they came back a few moments later.

'Where have they gone?' whispered Ronald.

'They can't have gone!' hissed Jeffrey. 'No one could get 'em away from here without a van.'

Bodkin and Matt watched them run off towards the kitchen.

The sound of their footsteps brought the policeman hurrying back. He blinked with astonishment. Where were the television sets? Something very strange was going on inside Motley and he was determined to get to the bottom of it. He was still trying to solve the mystery when Sir George came out of the library.

'And who might you be, sir,' said the policeman – looking straight at him.

There was a moment's pause. 'Can you see me?' gasped Sir George.

'See you, sir?' said the policeman, puzzled by Sir George's question. 'Oh yes, I can see you! I want to know what you're doing here!'

Chapter 6

IT was an awkward situation; it was obvious the policeman had no idea that Sir George was a ghost.

'He thinks Sir George is ... well ... flesh and blood,' whispered Bodkin to Matt. 'So it's up to Sir George to break it to him gently that he ain't. Then, once he's got the idea, Sir George can fade away. It's a little rule we made – just among ourselves. It's only polite really.'

Sir George walked over to the policeman and twirled his moustache. 'I'm General Uproar. General Sir George Uproar.' He pointed to the painting over the fireplace. 'That's me up there. Er – and down here too of course. Doesn't that tell you something?'

'No,' said the policeman stolidly.

'I lived here,' said Sir George somewhat impatiently. 'When would that be?'

'When would what be?'

'When you lived here,' said the policeman remorselessly.

Sir George was about to tell the policeman that he was a ghost when he thought better of it. He would have to explain things very carefully. The subject was a delicate one and he didn't want to frighten the wretched man more than necessary.

'The Uproars lived here for five hundred years – on and off – but mostly on. Humphrey was the last of us ...' Sir George paused significantly, but as the policeman didn't seem to understand what he was getting at, he thought he'd try a different approach. 'Did you know you have an unusual gift?' he said.

The policeman looked at him suspiciously. 'Are you trying to bribe me?'

'Certainly not!' snorted Sir George.

'Have you a key for this place?' asked the policeman.

'A key?'

'To get in and out,' said the policeman. 'How did you?'

'How did I what?'

'Get in and out!'

Sir George began thinking he was dealing with a lunatic. 'Gad, sir – through the door of course!' he said.

The policeman shook his head and smiled knowingly. 'I don't think you did.'

Sir George glared at him. 'I know I did!'

The policeman shook his head again. 'I think you came in through the window.'

'What! For fifty-eight years?' said Sir George.

'*Today*,' said the policeman. 'Because both the front and back doors are locked.'

'If that's so,' said Sir George, 'how did you get in?'

'A window at the back has been broken.'

'By whom?'

'Ah ... ha,' said the policeman. 'I was hoping you might tell me that. If you didn't come in through the window, how did you get in?'

Sir George sighed. 'You've got to know sooner or later, I suppose. I only hope the shock isn't going to be too much for you.'

'I shouldn't think so.'

Sir George prepared to vanish. 'Before I disappear, I –'

'I'll tell you when you can go, sir,' said the policeman firmly. 'You just tell me how you got in.'

'I didn't get in,' said Sir George, controlling himself with a great effort. 'I was here all the time.'

The policeman sat down on the tea-chest and took off his helmet. He was a patient man and determined to get at the truth. Somewhere in Motley Hall there were eight television sets and he was going to find them however long it took. 'Now then, sir,' he said patiently. 'When I first saw you, you seemed to be looking for something.'

Sir George beamed at him. 'Indeed I was. Mind you, I don't know what they're called, but I had a wonderful view until some fool of a woman started making a cake in front of the stands.'

'Cake?' said the policeman scratching his head. 'Stands?'

'No, not cake-stands!' said Sir George. 'The stands at the race-meeting, dammit! Do pay attention, officer! Anyhow I thought I'd better get another one.'

Sir George's garbled account only confused the policeman further. 'Get another what?' he asked wearily.

'Tatty-something or other,' said Sir George, searching for the word.

The policeman consulted his notebook. Things were beginning to make sense again. 'Tatyama,' he read.

'That's it!' said Sir George.

'Eight battery portable fully transistorized Tatyama television sets stolen from Stebbing's shop in Long Bolding High Street last week,' read the policeman.

'Stolen!' exclaimed Sir George.

'Now come on, sir,' said the policeman. 'Don't pretend you're not involved. Where have you hidden them?'

Jeffrey and Ronald peered round the door at the policeman. He was talking to himself and waving an admonishing finger at the air. As they couldn't see or hear Sir George, they came to the conclusion that the policeman was as mad as a hatter.

'Where have you hidden them?' the policeman repeated.

'He's cuckoo,' whispered Jeffrey.

'Gad,' roared Sir George, 'I haven't hidden them. I don't want 'em, and I wish I'd never seen 'em!'

The policeman leapt to his feet. 'Ah! So you *have* seen 'em?'

Sir George sighed. 'Of course I have. They've been here for days.'

He made a tremendous effort to disappear. His face grew purple and he quivered all over while the policeman looked at him anxiously. 'What are you doing?' he asked.

'That's my business,' panted Sir George, supporting himself against the billiard table.

The policeman was alarmed at the old gentleman's appearance. Sir George looked as if he might explode. 'Try to calm down,' he urged.

'Try to calm down?' roared Sir George. '*I'm trying to vanish!*'

Matt turned to Bodkin. 'Why can't he do it?' he asked.

Bodkin shrugged. 'I dunno. Must be something wrong with his ectoplasm.'

'I think you ought to sit down,' said the policeman.

Sir George ignored his advice. 'I don't want to sit down,' he shouted angrily.

'All right, all right,' said the policeman quickly, 'it was just an idea. But I'd stop trying to vanish if I were you. It can't be good for you.'

In the doorway, Jeffrey turned to Ronald. 'We can walk out of here any time we like. We can be goblins or fairies or anything. That policeman's balmy.'

'Don't you understand?' boomed Sir George. I'm an *emanation!*'

'You said you were a General!' said the policeman.

Sir George shook with rage. 'A shade – a spirit – a phantom!' he thundered. 'A ghost!'

The policeman was getting angry now. 'You think you can make a fool out of me, don't you?' he said. 'Well you can't! Now, where did you put those television sets?'

'By Balaclava! I am the ghost of Sir George Uproar! I've been dead for eighty years!' And once again Sir George tried to vanish.

'I wish you'd stop doing that!' said the policeman uneasily.

Sir George got his breath back and sat on the billiard table with a resigned expression. The policeman was obviously an idiot.

'You've seen things before, haven't you?' Sir George asked. 'Come now, you have, haven't you? There's no need to be ashamed of it. You must accept the fact, you're different!'

'I'm not,' said the policeman indignantly, beginning to sweat a little. 'There's nothing different about me. It's all a lot of imagination. That's what my Mum said.'

'Ah ha!' said Sir George, sensing he was getting

somewhere at last. 'Go – go on! What have you seen before?'

The policeman looked down at his boots and fiddled nervously with his notebook. 'I used to think I saw a little old man sitting on top of my wardrobe –'

Sir George leant forward. 'Tell me more,' he whispered.

The policeman went red. 'Well there was this nun in the cellar of the Admiral Nelson . . .'

Sir George sighed. 'You've got to know sooner or later, ing angrily, and the policeman backed away nervously. 'You saw this ridiculous old dodderer sitting on your wardrobe! You saw this miserable nun in a pub? Yet you refuse to believe in *me*?'

'Now just a minute –' the policeman began. But Sir George cut him short and pointed towards Ronald and Jeffrey, whom he had seen skulking in the shadows. 'There are the men who stole those thingummybobs!' he said.

The thieves were surprised when the policeman stopped talking to himself and suddenly looked in their direction. But anyone who held long conversations with invisible Generals was hardly likely to trouble them; so they strolled out of the shadows grinning broadly.

'And who might you two be?' demanded the policeman, looking at them suspiciously.

'I'm Napoleon and he's Henry V,' said Jeffrey.

The policeman groaned. 'They're as bad as you are,' he said to Sir George.

'Who's he?' asked Ronald politely.

'The ghost of Sir George Uproar,' answered the policeman wearily.

Jeffrey and Ronald sniggered.

'Now listen to me, you three lunatics,' he went on. 'It's no good trying to pull the wool over my eyes. You're all coming to the station.'

'I refuse!' rapped Sir George, who knew he couldn't anyway.

'You're coming!'

'Is he being difficult?' asked Jeffrey, suppressing his laughter.

'You heard what he said,' the policeman replied, beginning to lose his temper.

'Oh yes!' lied Jeffrey.

'You are the biggest idiot that it has been my misfortune to meet,' said Sir George to the policeman. 'These are the culprits! Why don't you arrest them?'

'As far as I'm concerned, you jokers are in this together.'

'Great Gladstone, man,' roared Sir George, 'they can't even *see* me! Go on! Ask them!'

'Er – can you see him?' the policeman asked Jeffrey and Ronald.

'Of course!' said Jeffrey.

'Ever so well!' said Ronald.

'Then where am I?' Sir George asked them. 'You see,' he said, turning to the policeman, 'they can't even *hear* me!'

The policeman looked curiously at the two thieves. They certainly didn't seem to have heard. And they weren't looking at Sir George either. There was only one logical explanation. All three of them were trying to drive him crazy.

Sir George suddenly became aware that his ability to vanish was returning. 'Have you ever heard the shortest ghost story in the world?' he asked the policeman.

'There were two gentlemen in a railway carriage. Strangers to each other. "Do you believe in ghosts?" says one of them –'

' "No," says the other,' finished the policeman. 'And vanished.'

'You've heard it before,' said Sir George. A triumphant smile spread across his face and he melted into thin air.

The policeman was staggered. He had been talking to a ghost after all! Jeffrey and Ronald took one look at his dazed expression and made a quick getaway.

'Why can't he see *us*?' whispered Matt to Bodkin.

'He only picks up Sir George's vibrations, I suppose,' muttered Bodkin. 'Let's get the magic boxes for him.'

As the policeman came out of his daze the secret passage opened and seven large boxes, apparently floating in mid air, formed a neat pile on the floor. A moment later Sir George reappeared with the television set from the Bell Tower.

'That's the lot,' he grunted. 'Take the wretched things away. They could become a very nasty habit.'

Chapter 7

TIME passed slowly for the ghosts of Motley Hall, and they were often very bored. This was because they knew each other too well and all their stories had become tedious through too much repetition. The monotony of their existence was partly responsible for all the bickering that went on, though even their quarrels had a pattern, and the wretched phantoms usually knew who was going to speak next and what they were going to say.

The only one of them who was still a bit of a mystery was the White Lady, and she steadfastly maintained she had no idea who she was. Bodkin didn't really believe her. He felt she was hiding something. Perhaps her past held a secret so dark and terrible she was forced to keep it to herself.

The excitement caused by the television sets was short-lived, and the ghosts soon settled back into the dull routine of being earthbound. Sir George went on writing his memoirs; the White Lady practised moaning and howling in the cellars; Fanny improved his swordsmanship; and Bodkin began teaching Matt to play the recorder.

'I think you're sucking instead of blowing,' he remarked sadly one afternoon as Matt staggered squeakily through 'Greensleeves'.

Everyone had played a musical instrument in Bodkin's day: recorders, viols, lutes and sackbuts. His friend Will Shakespeare had played a wiggly thing called a serpent which sounded like a bad attack of wind and had all the actors at the Globe helpless with laughter.

'And of course, everybody could sing in those days,' said Bodkin, and sang:

> 'Eliza is the fairest queen,
> That ever trod upon this green,
> Eliza's eyes are like the stars,
> Inducing peace, subduing wars.'

Matt clapped loudly and Bodkin swept off his cap and bowed low. 'I wrote that for the Queen's visit but she never arrived on account of her varicose veins,' he explained. 'Sir Richard was furious because the fireworks cost him a fortune. He loved fireworks. We were always having 'em at Motley. I remember the night a big rocket shot into the maze and flushed out Lord Beresford and a couple of milkmaids – sparks flying all over the place! A most amazing sight it was –' Bodkin paused. 'A *maze* in,' he repeated. 'It's a pun.'

Matt didn't think it was a very good pun, and had just begun playing 'Greensleeves' again when Sir George appeared suddenly on the billiard table. 'I have made an important discovery!' he announced.

'You haven't found Sir Peveril's treasure, have you, Sir George?' Matt asked excitedly.

The General shook his head and blew a shattering call to arms on an old bugle he carried slung round his neck by his Old Harrovian tie. The White Lady and Fanny appeared immediately. Fanny had drawn his sword, convinced they were being attacked, but when he saw no danger threatened he sheathed it again, and lolled nonchalantly against the fireplace.

'Do you have to make that revolting noise?' asked the White Lady coldly.

Sir George waved a book at her. 'As you all know,' he boomed pompously, 'I am writing my memoirs, and I was in the cellars just now, rummaging around for some old letters of mine, when I came across this.' He held up the book. 'It's Sacheverell Uproar's *History of Motley*. A fascinating work – absolutely fascinating. It devotes five pages to me, although, mind you, it's not terribly accurate. It says I was buried in Bognor. Anyway, to cut a long story short –'

'That would be nice –' the White Lady murmured.

'According to Sacheverell, this year marks the four hundredth anniversary of the founding of Motley Hall.' Sir George paused and waited for their reaction to this astounding piece of news. 'The four hundredth anniversary!' he repeated. 'What's the matter with you? Don't you understand? There should be some kind of ceremony.'

'What about a party?' said Matt.

'Oh, yes!' said Fanny. 'We could play lots of games.'

'And we could dance,' added the White Lady.

Sir George shook his head. 'I feel that the idea of us cavorting about with paper hats on is a bit bizarre in our ... er ... present circumstances. It would surely be more fitting if I were to unveil a memorial tablet with a suitable inscription.'

'Motley Hall – a symbol of England,' the White Lady suggested.

'None too safe and needs quite a bit of work doing on it,' added Bodkin with a grin. This jibe annoyed Sir George, who remarked indignantly that although Bodkin was always ready to mock he rarely had anything constructive to say. This was very unfair, for the Fool was the most practical of all the ghosts in Motley.

'We could do a masque,' Bodkin said tentatively.

The others looked puzzled. 'A masque is a kind of play,' he explained. 'With music and dancing and things. We could do *The Masque of Motley, Scenes from the History of a Famous House.*'

Fanny thought this was a splendid idea, and the ghosts got very enthusiastic. Then Sir George reminded them there would be nobody to watch it. The White Lady said she was sure they weren't the only ghosts in Motley, and though she approved of the masque she was worried they might offend someone.

'Well, if we do, we'll give 'em their money back!' grinned Bodkin.

He told them that when he was Fool to Sir Richard Uproar he had arranged several masques. He had written *Neptune's Darling* to celebrate Drake's voyage round the world, and *The Triumph of Gloriana over Venus, Minerva and Sir Richard Uproar* for the Queen's visit; and although Elizabeth's varicose veins had prevented her attendance the masque had still been performed. 'At least, until the accident put a stop to it,' he added.

'What accident?' asked the White Lady.

Bodkin smiled. 'Well, there was this lad, you see, playing Cupid. A nice boy he was, but a bit nervous. Naturally, being Cupid, he had a little bow, and an arrow which was quite sharp. Well, just as Sir Richard was bowing low before Venus, and reciting a long poem in her praise, Cupid's hand slipped and the arrow got Sir Richard right in the middle of his ... er ... speech.

'You've never seen anything like it,' he chuckled. 'Sir

Richard bellowed like a bull and grabbed the club I was holding – I was playing Hercules – and began chasing Cupid round Mount Olympus with me following on ... er ... behind, you might say, trying to pull out the arrow. At last Cupid took refuge in Venus' Flowery Bower, but Sir Richard smashed it to pieces with the club.

' "Mercy!" yells Cupid. "Hellhound!" thunders Sir Richard. "Stand still!" says I – still tugging away. It was pandemonium! Then suddenly – out comes the arrow and back I tumble over Mount Olympus to land smack on the top of Venus!

'Well, of course, we couldn't go on after that. I was laughing too much and Venus was winded, and most of the scenery had been wrecked by Sir Richard.' Bodkin smiled. 'All the same, I wish the Queen had seen it.'

After the laughter had died down, Sir George said he hoped they wouldn't need a Cupid in *The Masque of Motley*.

'We need a few allegorical figures,' the White Lady insisted.

'Do we?' said Fanny, wondering what an allegorical figure was.

'If I'm to write this masque,' said Bodkin, 'there's only one allegorical figure needed. And as I've been in Motley longer than any of you, I shall play him.'

'Play who?' asked Sir George.

'Time,' said Bodkin.

But it took him much longer to write the masque than he had anticipated. One particular problem was that he couldn't remember what had happened to Ebenezer Uproar during the Civil War. Ebenezer had changed sides so often that in the end everyone had been after him, and Bodkin couldn't remember whether he was finally caught by the Parliamentarians or the Royalists. When he tried looking it up in the *History of Motley*, he found that someone had torn out some of the pages.

'Why would anyone do that?' asked the White Lady when he confronted the other ghosts.

'Perhaps Ebenezer did it,' suggested Fanny. 'He might have come back specially.'

'To stop me writing about him?'

The others nodded.

'No,' Bodkin said. 'That's not like Ebenezer. From what I remember, he was about as sensitive as a pewter mug.'

'I can't see that it matters very much,' said the White Lady, with a sniff.

But Bodkin didn't like people tearing bits out of books. 'It's ruined the *History of Motley*,' he said. 'And it also means we'll have to leave all the Civil War stuff out of the masque.'

'We could have another song instead,' suggested Fanny.

Bodkin groaned, because he knew he would have to write it.

'I'm sure you'll think of something,' said Sir George patronizingly.

'You sound just like Burbage,' said Bodkin bitterly. 'He was always saying that. I remember when Will was writing *Hamlet*, and didn't know how to finish it. "I'm sure you'll think of something," said Burbage. "How about a nice death scene?" "Excellent!" says Will, with a wicked gleam in his eye. "We'll have one in your dressing-room after the play!"'

The mystery of the missing pages was unlikely to be solved that afternoon, so Bodkin handed out what he had written so far, and the ghosts prepared to rehearse.

The masque began with Queen Elizabeth knighting Sir Richard Uproar. The White Lady was Queen Elizabeth while Sir George played his illustrious ancestor. Bodkin placed his actors and the rehearsal began.

'What do I do?' asked Fanny.

'Try to look interesting,' Bodkin told him. 'You're Essex.'

'Essex who?'

'The Earl of Essex, you great hoddy-doddy!'

'How will anyone know that?'

The White Lady looked up from her script. 'Because I call you Essex. I say so. Listen:

"Essex come hither, hand to me my sword." '

Fanny studied his script. 'Oh yes, I see,' he murmured. 'And do I?'

'Do you what?' Bodkin asked.

'Hand to her my sword.'

'Well, of course you do, you ninny,' Bodkin shouted, exasperated at Fanny's stupidity. 'She can't knight him without one, can she?'

'Ain't she got one of her own? Od's bud – she's the Queen, ain't she?'

Sir George joined in the argument. 'I think Fanny's right, Bodkin. I do feel Queen Elizabeth would have her own sword for knighting people.'

'Well, she didn't,' Bodkin retorted. 'She borrowed one from the Earl of Essex.' He thumped the book. 'It says so in here.'

'It also says I was buried at Bognor!' exclaimed Sir George, beginning to bridle.

'Oh, get on with it!' ordered Bodkin rudely.

'Don't adopt that tone with me, sir!' said Sir George clasping his hands behind his back and pushing out his chin aggressively.

'Fish-hooks!' said Bodkin. He nodded to the White Lady. 'Begin at: "Good sir –"'

> 'Good sir, you something decomposed appear,'

the White Lady read in her most regal-sounding voice.

Bodkin clutched his head in his hands despairingly. *'Discomposed!'*

The White Lady gave him a withering look. 'It's your terrible writing,' she snapped.

> 'Good sir, you something *discomposed* appear.
> I pray there's naught that can afright you here.'

There was a pause. It was Sir George's turn, but he'd been so impressed by the White Lady's delivery, he'd lost his place. The White Lady gave him a nudge. 'Go on,' she whispered.

Sir George cleared his throat noisily.

> 'Majesty, madam, is a thing divine.'

he bellowed.

'You don't have to shout,' said Bodkin, wondering if *The Masque of Motley* was such a good idea after all.

While the ghosts rehearsed, Matt whispered to Bodkin that he had thought of a plan which might help them to find out who had torn the pages from the book. Bodkin listened, and nodded his approval. Then surreptitiously he gave the boy the damaged book, and Matt crept out unobserved.

'Essex come hither, hand to me thy sword,'

said the White Lady with a grand gesture.

Fanny, bored at having nothing to say, was counting the bannister rails on the staircase.

'*Give her your sword!*' Bodkin yelled at him.

Fanny stopped counting the bannister rails, and quickly handed it over.

'Not like that,' groaned Bodkin. '*Kneeling down!*'

Fanny knelt at the White Lady's feet and offered up his sword. The White Lady took it, inclined her head graciously, and turned to Sir George.

'And Richard Uproar, kneel upon the sward,'

she read.

It was Sir George's turn to kneel down, but as Fanny had forgotten to get up the two figures found themselves kneeling side by side. Sir George glared at Fanny. 'You're not being knighted you fool!' he hissed. '*You're the Earl of Essex!*'

'But Bodkin told me to kneel down,' said Fanny.

'Just to hand her the sword, you great potato!' said Bodkin despairingly. 'Then you get up and back away.'

'You didn't say anything about getting up and backing away,' argued Fanny. 'You said –'

But before Fanny could get any further Matt ran up with the *History of Motley*. 'I can't read,' he said, 'but this looks just like that other book. The one about Motley. It's the same colour and everything.'

Bodkin took it from him. '*The History of Motley* by Sacheverell Uproar,' he read.

'Are there any pages missing?' asked Matt innocently.

Bodkin flipped quickly through the book. 'It doesn't look like it,' he said. 'Well, ain't that lucky! I'll be able to write about Ebenezer now.' And he smiled at the other ghosts.

Of course, Matt was only pretending he had found another copy, and after the rehearsal, Bodkin put the book carefully on the mantelpiece, hoping it would act as bait. Then he and Matt hid to see if anyone would come for it. 'There was something in it they don't want the rest of us to know about,' whispered Bodkin. 'That's why they tore it out.'

The two ghosts waited patiently and for a long time nothing happened. Then, just as they were about to give up, the White Lady appeared and hurried to the fireplace to examine the book. When she saw that the pages were missing, she realized she had been tricked. But it was too late.

'Boo!' said Bodkin.

Chapter 8

THE harder the ghosts tried to make the White Lady talk the more mulish she became, and in the end she sat with her arms folded and refused to answer any of their questions.

'Why did you come back for the book?' asked Bodkin for the umpteenth time.

'I was curious,' said the White Lady.

'Fish-hooks! Your story's as thin as a rasher of wind. You thought this was another copy, and you were going to fillet it.'

The White Lady looked at him with disdain. 'I'm not interested in your silly theories.'

'What's in the missing pages?'

'How should I know? They're missing.'

Sir George drummed his fingers impatiently on the billiard table. 'Let's start again!' he grunted.

'I don't want to start again,' the White Lady replied, rising from her chair. 'Such a ridiculous fuss over a few pages missing from a dreary book. A book nobody wants to read anyway!'

'Listen to me, madam,' roared Sir George, completely losing his temper.

'Don't you "madam" me, you puffed up blunderbuss! I refuse to be humiliated any longer.' The White Lady flounced up the stairs. 'And what's more you can get someone else for your silly masque because I'm not going to be in it!'

Sir George was the first to recover. 'She'll come back,' he muttered. 'She's just having another tantrum.'

But Bodkin wasn't so sure. He'd seen the White Lady in a temper before, but this was different. This time he felt she really meant it. It seemed *The Masque of Motley* was doomed: they certainly couldn't perform it without her.

'And I was so looking forward to being Sussex,' murmured Fanny.

'Essex!' Bodkin corrected irritably.

Sir George stood up, stretched, and flicked a speck of dust from his cuff. 'It's not knowing who she is,' he said. 'It makes her very irritable.'

'Perhaps she's found out,' said Matt.

Bodkin picked up the book. 'I think you've got it! Something in here told her who she is – I mean – was –'

While Sir George outlined a plan of action, Fanny crept away unnoticed. He had always liked the White Lady and didn't mind her waspish outbursts at all. Now he felt she needed a champion to defend her. Although Fanny was not very clever he had a generous nature and a strong sense of fair play. He guessed the White Lady would take refuge in the cellars so he went down there, hoping to persuade her to appear so that he could comfort her.

'I'm alone, White Lady,' he said quietly. 'But you don't have to appear unless you want to. That's if you're in here, of course.' He sat down on a rusty old tin trunk. 'I mean if you are not in here, you can't appear, can you?' He took off his wig in his embarrassment. 'It's just that, if you are here, I'm your very humble servant, ma'am, and resolved to help you in your misfortune.'

A white mist formed in front of him and slowly became the familiar outline of the White Lady.

'Go away!' she said. 'You've been sent by the others. I know you have.'

'No, I haven't. I swear it!'

'Can I trust you?'

'Absolutely.'

'You won't tell them anything?'

'Certainly not,' said Fanny.

The White Lady went to a tattered roll of carpet felt, took the missing pages from it, and handed them to Fanny with a theatrical gesture. 'I've found out who I am!' she said.

'Are you famous?' asked Fanny.

'In a way.'

'Seventeenth century?'

'Yes.'

'The Uproar family?'

'No.'

'Related?'

'No.'

'Connected?'

'Yes.'

There was a pause. 'How many have I had so far?' asked Fanny, who had somehow started playing Twenty Questions.

'This isn't a game, you idiot!' said the White Lady irritably. 'It was a terrible shock to me when I opened the book and found this.'

Fanny gasped. He was looking at a picture of the White Lady. 'Lady Perfidia Blackart,' he read.

'And what do you say to that?' said the White Lady dramatically.

Fanny didn't really know. 'Er –' he stammered. 'I've always thought of you as an Emma.'

The White Lady paced restlessly round the cellars, wringing her hands. 'I am Lady Blackart! The *infamous* Lady Blackart!'

'Infamous?' repeated Fanny, alarmed to see the White Lady so distressed.

'No wonder I could never remember who I was,' she sobbed. 'No wonder I'm earthbound and doomed to walk for ever within Motley's walls – walls endlessly echoing with the cries of my *victims*!'

'Victims?' gulped Fanny. He backed away nervously and fell over a broken rabbit hutch.

'Those pages told me everything,' the White Lady went on. 'How I worked for Cromwell. How he sent me on a dreadful mission. How I arrived at Motley whilst great flashes of lightning rent the heavens and the wind and rain howled round the house. Howled and sobbed like the souls of the damned.'

Fanny was beginning to wish that he hadn't come.

'Shall I go on?' said the White Lady.

'If you must,' he said faintly. 'But I shan't sleep.'

'I told them I'd lost my way, that I was loyal to the King. "Come in, come in," said Ebenezer. "You must be chilled to the very bone."

'I smiled at the treacherous dog and his brood as we sat down to supper.'

'What brood?'

'His wife and ten children,' said the White Lady impatiently, and then returned to her grand manner. 'Before dawn, I would scotch this nest of vipers!'

Fanny was horrified. 'You didn't, did you?'

The White Lady nodded grimly. 'A hollow ring

containing poison!' she explained. 'As the servant finished pouring the wine into my goblet I pretended to
steady the flagon and secretly dropped in the fatal
tincture.'

'The f-f-fatal t-t-tincture?'

'But my plan misfired. Unknown to me, young Henry
Uproar changed his goblet for mine, and thus became
the only survivor.' The White Lady paused. 'And I was
killed with my own poison.'

Fanny took a large silk handkerchief from his pocket
and wiped his ghostly brow. 'And you remembered
nothing about all this until you read it in the book?'

'Nothing,' said the White Lady.

'No wonder you tore it out.'

The White Lady looked searchingly at him. 'I still
haven't told you the worst.'

'Od's bud! What could be worse?'

'Apparently I go peculiar at the full moon,' she said,
showing him one of the missing pages.

'It is said that Lady Blackart committed all her
crimes when the moon was full,' Fanny read. Then he
looked up at the White Lady. 'You've never gone
peculiar at the full moon,' he said. 'Not particularly
peculiar anyway.'

'Ah, but I didn't know I was Lady Blackart then,
did I? It's going to make a big difference. We'll soon be
able to put it to the test. There's a full moon tonight!'

Fanny pleaded with her to tell the others everything
and tried to persuade her they would understand. He
pointed out that her life as Lady Blackart had been
three hundred years ago. However, despite his eloquent
entreaties, the White Lady eventually melted away into

the dusty air. She had heard Sir George and the others hurrying down to the cellars, and Fanny was still staring at where she had vanished, when they burst in and grabbed the missing pages from him.

'By Jove! How ghastly!' muttered Sir George, as he read them 'The Massacre at Motley'.

'No wonder she's earthbound,' said Matt.

'It's come as a dreadful shock to her,' said Fanny, determined to defend her.

'It hasn't done *me* any good!' said Bodkin.

'The woman's a *monster*!' breathed Sir George.

'Poppycock!' exclaimed Fanny. 'We got on very well with her before we knew who she was. I can't see that a name makes that much difference.'

'It does when it's Perfidia Blackart!' said Bodkin.

But Matt was on Fanny's side. He didn't think it mattered who the White Lady had been. Just because she'd discovered her past why should it change how they felt about her? 'Live and let live,' he said.

'A singularly inappropriate motto, if I may say so,' said Sir George.

The ghosts were divided on this issue and there seemed no way to resolve their differing viewpoints. After a sharp exchange Bodkin and Sir George left the cellars.

'This is ridiculous,' said the White Lady, when she reappeared moments later. 'I have as much right to be here as they have. I didn't ask to be Lady Perfidia, did I?'

Back in the Great Hall, Bodkin picked up the *History of Motley* and hurled it against the wall. Pages fluttered all over the place. 'A fine four hundredth anniversary this is turning out to be!' he muttered angrily. 'No Masque! Perfidia Blackart! And the rest of us fighting among ourselves.'

He looked up to see the White Lady coming slowly down the stairs, and he moved away nervously.

'It's all right,' she said disdainfully. 'I'm not going to attack you!'

'We'll make sure of that, Lady Blackart,' said Sir George, very much on the defensive.

'Are you coming quietly?' said Bodkin.

'I always come quietly,' said the White Lady. 'Anyway, I'm giving myself up. Why should I skulk in draughty corners, waiting for you two to hunt me down.' She looked fondly at Fanny and Matt. 'At least I know who my real friends are. I shall stay in the cellars if that will make you happier.'

'No,' cried Fanny. 'I won't allow it.'

'I've made up my mind,' she said as she walked slowly towards the cellar door. 'As a matter of fact I think I shall prefer it!' Then with a final wave to Matt and Fanny, she went bravely down into the cellars.

There was a long unhappy silence. The White Lady's courageous self-banishment had impressed all of them. Now they began to realize just how much they were going to miss her.

'It will seem very odd without her,' said Fanny sadly. 'There won't be any more bridge parties.'

Bodkin tried to hide his feelings by clearing up the pages of the ruined book. Something in one of them puzzled him and he began to read more closely. Then he turned to Sir George. 'What does errata mean?' he asked.

'Latin,' said Sir George, still sadly thinking about the White Lady, 'it means errors or mistakes.'

'Well, I think we've just made a big one,' replied Bodkin with great excitement. 'Listen to this: "Errata. The picture on page 212 is not that of Lady Blackart. Lady Blackart's portrait is to be found facing page 258."'

While the full meaning of this was still being grasped, Bodkin rushed to the cellar door and called loudly into the darkness. 'You're not Perfidia Blackart,' he shouted. 'And what's more – you never have been.'

At length Bodkin came running back with the White Lady, and everyone started talking at once, each trying to tell her why she wasn't Perfidia Blackart, and how the mistake had been made. The White Lady was dazed and bewildered. 'But it says Perfidia Blackart under my picture,' she murmured.

'Don't you understand? The picture's wrongly titled!' Bodkin explained.

The White Lady looked anxiously at the others and they all nodded reassuringly. The idea of being Lady Perfidia Blackart for ever had filled her with horror. She had found it impossible to believe she had done all those dreadful things to the Uproar family. But something still troubled her. 'If I'm not her – who am I?' she asked. 'It must say *something* about my picture.'

Sir George read the errata page again. 'The picture on page 212 should now be titled –'

'Go on,' she begged. 'Go on! Who am I?'

Sir George looked at her sadly. '. . . should now be titled – "Portrait of an Unknown Lady",' he read.

Chapter 9

SOMETHING very odd was moving slowly across the Great Hall. Matt watched it curiously from the balcony. He had certainly not seen it before, and he had seen some very strange things in Motley since his first visit. The apparition was accompanied by a clanking of chains and some rather miserable groans. The image was too indistinct to make out any particular features, and after a moment or two it faded away completely.

Fanny, who was asleep on the billiard table, complained bitterly when Matt woke him up to tell what he had seen. Fanny had been dreaming of being alive again and wasn't at all interested. He turned over and went back to sleep, hoping to renew his dream. Bodkin, too, was more concerned with writing a new madrigal than with hearing about Matt's strange experience. Finally, Matt found Sir George in the Orangery, where he was boring the White Lady with the latest chapter of his memoirs.

'There were thousands of them,' he was saying. 'All yelling like demons and banging their spears against their shields. "What are we going to do?" said young Chudleigh-Watson. "Stand and fight," I said –'

'Wasn't that a little foolhardy?' interrupted the White Lady.

Sir George looked at her. 'Oh no – he wasn't there.'

'Who wasn't there?' asked the White Lady.

'That little fool, Hardy,' said Sir George. 'I got rid of him. Sent him on leave. Best place for him. The little beggar was more trouble than he was worth. Where was I?'

'Facing thousands of Fuzzy-Wuzzies,' said the White Lady, doing her best not to yawn.

'Ah yes,' said Sir George. ' "Stand and fight," I said, "That's what we're going to do. We'll show these savages how Englishmen can die!" '

'And did you?' asked the White Lady.

'Oh yes, it was an absolute massacre. In fact, only about ten of us survived.' Sir George paused uncomfortably. 'Mind you, the ammunition had quite a lot to do with it.'

'Why was that?'

'It was the wrong size. It wouldn't go in the rifles.'

'Whose fault was that?' asked the White Lady.

Sir George turned and looked out of the window. 'I think we're in for some more rain,' he muttered.

'I've just seen something in the Great Hall, Sir George,' said Matt. 'Groaning and clanking. I tried to tell Bodkin and Fanny about it but they wouldn't listen. It were like chains rattling or summat. And it moaned a bit, as well.'

'It couldn't be Old Gory, could it?' the White Lady asked Sir George anxiously.

'Surely not,' he replied. 'He can't be due yet. It seems only yesterday he was here last.'

'Time flies, Sir George,' sighed the White Lady.

Sir George nodded. 'And we're not getting any younger.'

'Or older . . .'

'True . . .'

'Who's Old Gory?' asked Matt, sensing the two of them were sinking into a despondent mood.

Sir George explained that Old Gory was a ghost who had been haunting there even before Motley had been built. A fierce battle had been fought there during the Wars of the Roses and Old Gory had been slain. It was lucky for the permanent phantoms of Motley that he only appeared every five years, because he was the most miserable apparition in the whole supernatural world.

When Bodkin and Fanny were warned that they could expect a visit from Old Gory they got very depressed.

'I can't stand that old moaner,' muttered Bodkin. 'All he does is complain. He's completely wrapped up in himself and expects us to sit round and sympathize. And he's so *visible*!'

'Visible!' repeated Matt. 'I could hardly see him!'

'You wait till he really appears,' Bodkin warned. 'He's one of those conspicuous spectres. Everyone sees him. Not only us, but people as well!'

Sir George remembered he had seen Old Gory on several occasions during his own lifetime. So had his father and his grandfather.

'And your great-great-grandfather,' said Fanny.

'My governess even did a charcoal sketch of him,' Sir George added.

'The really distressing thing about Old Gory,' said the White Lady, 'is that he won't go away. He hangs around for days.'

'Well, he was here first, wasn't he?' said Matt. 'I mean you'd be miserable if you knew you weren't welcome. Perhaps if we were all a bit more friendly we might cheer him up.'

'I'd rather cheer up a funeral,' said Bodkin glumly.

'You could tell him some of your jokes,' Matt suggested.

'We don't want him bursting into tears,' said the White Lady acidly.

'That old meacock was born miserable,' said Bodkin. 'He died miserable and he's *still* miserable. And nothing we can do will change that!'

Suddenly the White Lady struck a dramatic pose. 'Hark!' she exclaimed, in her grandest manner, 'a rattling of chains! He is nigh!'

'Fish-hooks!' said Bodkin. 'Someone's unlocking the front door!'

The ghosts melted into the shadows as the front door opened and Mr Jack Potter walked in. He was a big red-faced man and he wore a polo-neck sweater and corduroy trousers. Behind him staggered his wife carrying a couple of suitcases.

'Careful with those, Margaret!' said Potter, as she dropped her heavy burdens with relief. 'Don't just bang them down any old where.'

'They're very heavy, Jack,' said Mrs Potter, making a statement rather than a complaint.

'No they're not!' replied her husband heartlessly. 'Let's get the rest of the stuff.' He stalked out to the car with his hands in his pockets and Mrs Potter followed him, still trying to get her breath back.

'Has he bought Motley?' asked Bodkin.

'I hope not!' said the White Lady, who didn't like the way Mr Potter treated his wife.

'They don't look the sort that can see us,' said Fanny.

'You never can tell,' said Sir George cautiously. 'It's as well to be on the safe side.' He knew from experience that the most unlikely people saw ghosts.

They watched curiously as the Potters returned with another heap of luggage. Mr Potter brought a small camera with him, while Mrs Potter lugged in two more suitcases and some heavy-looking cardboard boxes.

'It's grand,' said Potter, admiring all the cobwebs while his wife sat down to recover. 'Just what I've been looking for. It's been empty for over twenty years. We'd go a long way to find a better place than this, Margaret.'

'They *are* buying it,' whispered the White Lady.

'It seems a shame really,' panted Mrs Potter. 'Almost as though we're trespassers.'

Potter ignored his wife's comment and rummaged in the cardboard boxes. 'Where are the thermometers?' he asked.

'I know I packed them,' said his wife anxiously.

'Well, where are they? You can't lose forty-eight thermometers!'

The ghosts looked at one another. 'Forty-eight thermometers?' repeated Sir George wonderingly.

'Perhaps he's starting a hospital,' the White Lady suggested.

Potter found the thermometers and wandered round the Great Hall with a handful of them. He placed two on the mantelpiece and carefully propped others against the walls. Then he took some table-tennis balls and after placing them at random on the stairs he drew little circles round them with a piece of chalk.

'I don't think he's very well,' said the White Lady.

Potter stepped back to admire the effect and asked his wife what she thought. Mrs Potter replied that it looked very nice and then continued knitting some baby clothes for her daughter-in-law.

'I wish you'd show a little more interest,' said Potter, tying a piece of cotton across the stairs. 'I'm going to get one! I can feel it in my bones.'

'What's the lunatic doing now?' asked Fanny.

Next, Potter took some tiny bells from his pocket and hooked them along the cotton like washing on a line. He made sure that they tinkled nicely and then asked his wife for talcum powder.

'It's lavender,' she said, producing a blue tin from a crumpled carrier bag.

'It doesn't matter what it smells like!' exclaimed Potter, grabbing it from her. He sprinkled the talcum powder all over the stairs, which gave them rather a wintry look, and this, together with the little bells and the ping-pong balls, made the staircase look quite like Christmas.

'That'll rule out any hanky-panky!' said Potter, very pleased with the result. 'Anything that comes down these stairs and doesn't move anything *will be a ghost*.'

The ghosts were astounded.

'And I shall photograph it,' Potter went on, 'however long it takes. The moment the temperature drops,' Potter waved vaguely at the thermometers, 'I shall know they're here. You need a lot of patience, Margaret.'

'Yes, dear,' said Mrs Potter with a sigh, wishing she'd chosen a simpler knitting pattern.

'It's a very unusual hobby is ghost-hunting,' said Potter. 'Very unusual.'

'Oh, I know,' said Mrs Potter, her needles clicking away like mad. 'But then, you've had so many unusual hobbies, haven't you, Jack? And they never seem to last.'

Potter grunted and carefully screwed his camera on its tripod.

'I didn't mind the radio-controlled model aeroplanes,'

said his wife. 'What came after that? Oh yes – breeding performing seals . . .'

Potter paid no attention to her. Instead, he focused his camera on the snowy-looking staircase, collected some more ping-pong balls and thermometers and marched off down the corridor humming loudly.

'A ghost hunter!' exclaimed Sir George indignantly. 'I've never heard of anything more disgraceful! It makes one feel like some sort of rare beetle!'

'He only wants a few pictures!' said Fanny, who felt Sir George was getting unnecessarily agitated.

'Great Gladstone, man! Can you imagine what would happen if he did manage to photograph us?'

'He'd go away, wouldn't he?' Bodkin suggested.

Sir George shook his head. 'He'd want more and more pictures! Portraits and family groups! Informal studies! "The White Lady and Friend". "Sir George in Pensive Mood". Well, I absolutely refuse to have my picture splashed across some ghastly newspaper!'

'Not even *The Times*?' said the White Lady.

'Not even the *Church Times*!'

The White Lady looked doubtfully at him. 'I think you're being a little over-sensitive,' she said. 'After all, in a sense we would be helping to ... er ... push back the frontiers of knowledge.'

'Then you can push 'em back without me! Make no mistake, Madam, if we let this lout have his way, in no time at all the place will be positively *crawling* with ghost hunters. It will hail little white balls. There will be great drifts of talcum powder all over the place. Bells everywhere! And whenever we appear, we'll face dozens of sensation-seeking scallywags, each eager to –'

'All right! All right! You've made your point,' broke

in Bodkin, weary of Sir George's stream of rhetoric. It was useless merely talking about it; something practical had to be done. However, the ghosts were still seeking an answer to this latest menace when Mr Potter ran back to his wife in a state of high excitement.

'I've found a corridor like an ice-box!' he told her. 'It just has to be haunted, Margaret! Come on, woman! Come and see!'

So Mrs Potter folded her knitting and wearily followed her enthusiastic husband.

Immediately the Potters had gone, the ghosts heard the sound of chains being dragged across the floor, and a white blur appeared before them and slowly became the shadowy figure of an armed man. He wore a tattered leather jerkin over rusty chain-mail. His ankles were manacled and from them trailed short pieces of chain which made the clanking sound Matt had heard. From his belt hung a long sword, its blade hacked and blunt.

But the most unusual thing about Old Gory was his head. Instead of keeping it in the usual place for heads, he carried it under one arm. The head wore a battered helmet with the visor up and a miserable face peered out, like an ancient scorpion-fish.

'Well, don't look so pleased to see me, will you?' it moaned.

Chapter 10

OLD Gory's body clanked up and down the Great Hall while Sir George and the others followed him and awkwardly tried to engage the head in conversation.

'How have you been keeping?' asked Sir George.

'I ain't bin well,' the head answered. 'Not at all well.'

'What's the trouble?' inquired Bodkin, wishing that Old Gory was anywhere except in Motley Hall.

'I get these terrible headaches,' replied Old Gory.

'What sort of headaches?' asked Sir George.

'Eh?'

Bodkin bent down and shouted at the head. '*What sort of headaches?*'

'Splittin' headaches,' it answered. 'And that's not all –'

'I didn't think it would be,' muttered Bodkin.

'The wound in me leg keeps playin' up. Sometimes I think I'll never walk again.' The body stopped marching and the helmeted head rolled its eyes up at Bodkin. 'You'd like that, wouldn't yer?' it said mournfully.

'Oh, don't be ridiculous!' said Sir George.

'Ridiculous,' repeated Old Gory's head. 'Yes, I was waiting for that! In fact I was expecting it. That's what you think of me, ain't it? A ridiculous old man, who's no use any more. A burden. A nuisance. Oh yes I know . . . !'

It was the most depressing voice imaginable. Querulous, bad-tempered and full of self-pity. It reminded Matt of the stable-door creaking in the wind.

'We weren't expecting you so soon,' said Sir George, controlling himself with an effort.

'Eh?'

'*I said, we weren't expecting you so soon!*'

'Oh, weren't you!' said Old Gory.

Sir George was tired of walking up and down bent practically double while he tried to put the tiresome old ghost at his ease. 'Can't you stop this excessive perambulation?' he said.

'I'm on sentry-go,' whined the head. 'You ought to know that by now – and you being a General. You see? I get no understanding. No consideration. No sympathy.'

'I could strangle him!' whispered Bodkin to the White Lady.

'How?' she replied.

'Come and sit down, old chap,' said Sir George, doing his very best to remain polite.

'I don't want to sit down! I don't want no favours from any of you. And I ain't going to be treated like an invalid.'

'Of course not,' Sir George agreed. 'We merely want you –'

'I know what you say about me when I ain't here, so don't you think I don't,' the peevish and monotonous voice continued.

'We're always very pleased to see you – aren't we?' appealed Sir George.

'Always,' said Bodkin.

'Delighted,' said the White Lady, with a frigid little smile.

Old Gory's head glared at them. 'You won't get round me with a lot of cant. I've suffered nothing but indifference and neglect at your hands. The mortification I've endured! Oh, the wretched depths of my misery!'

'Oh, Gloriana!' muttered Bodkin.

'You mustn't give way like this,' said Sir George. 'Isn't there anything we can do to cheer you up?'

'I don't want to be cheered up.'

'I was afraid of that,' said Bodkin.

'How are we going to get rid of him?' whispered Sir George.

'Well, for a start,' muttered Bodkin, 'it's no use being nice to him. It'll only make him worse. The more you try cheering him up the gloomier he's going to get. Why don't we tell him what we *really* think of him. *Insult* him into going.'

'But he likes being insulted,' said the White Lady. 'It gives him an excuse for being miserable.'

'We've got to think of *something* to make him go,' said Sir George. 'If that wretched ghost hunter sees him, we're done for!'

'A photograph of Old Gory!' breathed Bodkin. 'Think of it!'

Sir George was horror-stricken. 'They'll run special trains!' he said.

Old Gory's body put his head down on the billiard table. The head looked over to where the ghosts were huddled together. 'What are you lot whispering about?' it said suspiciously.

Bodkin lost his temper. 'It's none of your business, you dreary old decapitation!' he shouted. 'You sit there – looking as if you won yourself at a fair – and expect us to put up with all your moaning and groaning –'

'That's right!' bleated the head piteously. 'Insult me!

You like doing that, don't you? Go on! Pour scorn on my affliction!'

'I'd like to pour boiling oil on it!' muttered Bodkin.

'Hear that? Did you hear what he said!' cried the head.

'You'd better be quiet, Bodkin,' said Sir George.

The rheumy old eyes swivelled round to Sir George. 'You're as bad. And so is that simpering shade over there. You'd all like to get rid of me, wouldn't you? Don't try to deny it! I'm nothing but a burden to you, ain't I? And me an old soldier what gave up his head for King and Country!'

'Balderdash!' roared Sir George, losing his patience completely.

'You see? I get nothing but harsh words and mockery every time I appear,' the head droned on relentlessly. 'And yet not once have I ever complained. I know my rights. If I want to haunt this place, there's nothing any of you can do to stop me.'

The ghosts knew this was true. If Old Gory wished to appear they could do nothing to stop him. Somehow they would have to persuade him to leave. Sir George decided to tell him everything in the hope that he might see reason. He sat down facing the head. 'Now look here, Gory, old boy,' he said, 'there's something you ought to know —'

Old Gory's eyes glittered angrily. 'Been keeping something from me, have you?'

'Keeping it from you?' groaned Bodkin. 'Why, you old bagpipe, we can hardly get a word in edgeways!'

'I ain't talking to you!' snapped Old Gory.

'Good,' said Bodkin, and retired to the fireplace.

Sir George spoke to the head again. 'There's someone in the house. A person. He's ... looking for ghosts.'

'Well, he might be lucky, mightn't he,' Old Gory replied.

'But he's a ghost *hunter*!' said Sir George desperately. 'With a ... er ... machine for making pictures. Pictures of *us*!'

'I see,' said Old Gory. 'You think *my* picture wouldn't be good enough!'

Sir George restrained himself with an effort. 'We don't want him to take *any* pictures. Don't you understand?'

'I understand all right. I'd spoil it for you, wouldn't I? Because I'm more ... *interesting*!'

'But a picture would bring hundreds of people to Motley,' explained Sir George. 'Surely, you don't want that, do you?'

'I don't care,' the old ghost replied. 'I only appear here every five years!'

'But dammit, man! What about us?'

'You'll have to get used to it,' sneered Old Gory.

Bodkin looked threateningly at the head on the billiard table. There seemed no way of getting through to the rusty old bucket. At any moment the Potters might return and if they did, they would surely see Old Gory. So while Sir George continued to argue, Bodkin dispatched Matt and Fanny to keep an eye on Mr Potter, telling them that the minute the ghost hunter looked like coming back they were to warn him. If necessary Old Gory would have to be forcibly removed before the Potters caught sight of him.

Fanny and Matt found Mr Potter still playing with his little thermometers, while his wife sat in a window seat and got on with her knitting.

'In all the books they say there's a sudden dramatic drop in the temperature when ghosts are about,' said Potter. 'And places where they appear are unusually cold. You have to admit this corridor's unusually cold, isn't it, Margaret?'

'So's our bedroom, Jack,' replied his wife calmly, 'but we've never seen a ghost in it.'

'Oh you are encouraging, aren't you?' said Potter sarcastically. 'Motley Hall has a reputation for being haunted. That's why I chose it.'

'Well, I hope you won't be disappointed, that's all,' rejoined Mrs Potter, 'like you were over that cinema organ.'

'Why did you have to bring that up?' said Mr Potter sulkily. 'I'd have finished it, if they'd sent me all the parts.'

'I wish you'd get rid of the parts they did send,' replied Mrs Potter, clicking away with her knitting needles. 'I've nowhere to put the vacuum cleaner.'

Matt and Fanny looked blankly at each other. The Potters' conversation was beyond them. Cinema organs and vacuum cleaners were not part of their world at all.

'It's typical of you, Margaret,' Potter went on. 'Here I am, about to make a real psychic breakthrough, and all you can think of is where to put your vacuum cleaner.'

Mrs Potter accepted the rebuke with her usual quiet resignation. She was used to her husband's hobbies and knew that his passion for ghost-hunting was likely to be as short-lived as everything else. Fanny wanted a closer look at a thermometer, so he crept towards Potter who had just picked one up.

'Oh my goodness!' exclaimed Potter as the thermometer registered a dramatic drop in temperature.

Matt quickly pulled Fanny away and the thermometer's reading returned to normal.

'It happened!' cried Potter. 'It happened! Now I'm sure I've chosen the right place. I'll get my pictures if I have to come to Motley every day!'

'Od's bud!' cried Fanny. 'What a thought!'

'I'm going to take some photographs of that staircase in the main hall,' said Potter enthusiastically.

'Quickly!' said Matt. 'Warn Sir George!'

Fanny nodded and sped back to the Great Hall.

The ghosts were so alarmed when they heard that Potter was on his way, that they simply grabbed Old Gory's body and rushed it into the library.

'Stop thieves! Stop!' the head yelled desperately.

Matt ran in a moment later and was puzzled to find the Great Hall empty. Where had the ghosts gone?

'Villains! Varlets! Bring back my body!' Old Gory's head shouted angrily from the billiard table.

'Where's the rest of you?' Matt asked it breathlessly.

'Scoundrels! Rogues! Ruffians!' raged the head.

'Shut up! They'll hear you!' said Matt.

'I want them to hear me!' yelled the head, so Matt picked it up and ran with it into the cellars. He was only just in time. Mr and Mrs Potter returned a moment later.

When Bodkin came out of the library to collect the rest of Old Gory he was shocked to find it had mysteriously vanished. He looked under the billiard table, and then ran back to the library, empty-handed, and told the others. There was a moment of total panic which was immediately quelled by Sir George. 'Keep calm!' he thundered, 'we musn't lose our heads!'

Meanwhile, in the cellar, Old Gory was still calling out pathetically. 'I'm lost, lost,' he howled.

'No, you're not!' said Matt, doing his best to calm him. 'Well, part of you ain't. Why don't you look on the bright side! It'll be much easier to find the big bit.'

But nothing could placate the infuriated head. 'Thieves!' it shouted wildly. 'Body-snatchers!' It made such a noise that Matt lost patience with it and slammed down the visor. Yells and howls could still be heard coming from the helmet.

'If you don't stop that noise,' said Matt, 'I promise you'll never see your body again.'

It was an unfortunate situation. Matt had the head and the rest of the ghosts were in charge of the body. How would Old Gory's two bits be reunited?

In the Great Hall the ghosts continued their desperate search, while Potter took photos of the staircase.

'It couldn't move on its own, could it?' Fanny asked, anxiously looking up the chimney.

'The Screaming Skulls of Hollow Manor can,' said the White Lady, who was a fund of supernatural information.

'Oh, can they?' said Fanny nervously, hoping that Hollow Manor was a long way from Motley Hall.

'Oh, yes! They float about all over the place,' said the White Lady. 'Screaming, of course.'

'Of course,' said Fanny.

The ghosts were still hunting for the head under the very nose of the ghost hunter when Matt looked round the cellar door. 'If you're looking for the head,' he told them, 'it's downstairs.'

'It would serve him right if we left it there,' said Sir George.

'Where's the body?' asked Matt.

'In the library,' Bodkin answered, but he was wrong. During the head-hunt the body had marched from the library unnoticed and clanked off down the corridor towards the Potters.

Matt fetched the helmeted head and showed it to the rest of them. 'Here he is,' he said. 'Seems to have gone very quiet, don't he?'

Bodkin eyed the helmet suspiciously. 'Are you sure he's still in there?'

'Have a look,' said Matt.

Bodkin raised the visor and the mournful face peered out at him.

'Are you goin' to be sensible from now on?' said Bodkin, threateningly.

'Where's the rest of me?' whispered Old Gory.

The ghosts took him to the library. It was a dreadful moment when they realized the body had walked off.

'I want my body back!' yelled Old Gory.

'Of course you do,' said Sir George, doing his best to calm him down. 'It's understandable. You must be very attached to it.' Sir George corrected himself. '*Were* very attached to it.'

'Attached to it?' the head shouted. 'It *belongs* to me!'

While Old Gory raved, and threatened them with fearful punishment if they didn't find his body, the ghosts thought of the awful consequences if it blundered upon the Potters and was photographed.

'It can't have gone far on its own, can it?' said Fanny fearfully.

'Search everywhere!' ordered Sir George, taking charge in his customary manner. 'Leave no ... er ... stone unturned. I'll stay and guard this thing,' and he slammed the visor shut to muffle the stream of abuse from Old Gory.

The White Lady ran through the festoon of little bells and up the talcum-powdered staircase without disturbing a thing. Not a single ping-pong ball moved. Not the tiniest tinkle was heard. Bodkin hurried to the Bell Tower, and Fanny and Matt ran to the Orangery.

They were only just in time. There was Mr Potter busily taking photographs, watched by his wife, while the headless ghost crept up behind them. Matt and Fanny seized it and dragged it out of sight before Potter had the chance to notice it.

At the Old Gory Reunion it was hard to say which bit was more relieved. The body cradled the head almost lovingly, and the head looked fondly at the protective arms. Old Gory had promised Sir George that once he was 'together again', he would leave at once, and, much to everyone's relief he kept to his bargain and began rapidly fading away.

'Just a moment,' said Matt. 'Does he have to carry his head?'

'What do you mean?' Fanny asked.

'Why doesn't he *wear* it?' Matt suggested.

'*Wear* it?' said the White Lady.

'Yes,' said Matt. 'On his shoulders!'

'I never thought of that!' said the head. Then, encouraged by the ghosts, Old Gory's body lifted his head and placed it between his shoulders. The ghosts were staggered at the transformation. He looked almost human!

'It's a distinct improvement,' said Sir George.

'Do you really think so?' said Old Gory rather shyly. 'It feels a bit wobbly.'

'It's bound to at first,' said Matt, 'but you can practise. After all, you've got five years before you put in another appearance!'

'Five years!' Old Gory repeated. 'So I have. Does it really look better?'

The ghosts assured him that it really had made a tremendous difference.

'It looks absolutely ... *capital*,' said Sir George with a smile.

'Then I'll see you in five years' time,' said Old Gory. 'Farewell!' and still with his head in the right place, the ancient ghost saluted them and faded from sight.

Matt's brilliant solution greatly impressed the ghosts and they all congratulated him warmly. 'Well,' he said modestly, 'you'd be miserable if you had your head in your hands all the time!'

But the ghosts' biggest surprise was yet to come. Mr Potter's enthusiasm for ghost hunting had waned during the course of the day, just as his wife had expected it would. He had found Motley Hall a chilly and disappointing place, and none of his experiments had yielded any results. So, resigned to failure, he packed up all his thermometers and table-tennis balls, and took down his little bells. The ghosts watched him leave with considerable relief. Then Mrs Potter returned to pick up her knitting and looked straight at them all standing on the staircase, and gave them a knowing smile. 'You'll be all right now,' she whispered. 'He's given up ghost hunting!' And before they could recover from their astonishment she went out, quietly closing the door behind her.

Chapter 11

WHENEVER there was a storm over Motley Hall the ghosts were irritable and easily upset. The heavy atmosphere depressed them, and they would each seek solitude in their own particular corner of the empty house. One such storm rolled around Motley Hall on an afternoon in late October. The flashes of lightning flickered at the rainswept windows and threw strange shadows on the walls. The sound of thunder tumbled through the house as Fanny came down the stairs with a leaking bucket and interrupted Sir George, who was still trying to finish his memoirs.

'I can't keep going up and down with this bucket,' Fanny complained. 'On my honour I can't. And the rain's coming in even harder!'

Sir George was furious he had been disturbed. 'Get Matt to help you,' he snapped.

'He's out,' said Fanny.

'Lucky little apparition,' muttered Sir George. 'I've never understood why he's able to go in and out while we are forced to remain indoors. We are not just earthbound – we're confined to barracks as well.'

'This bucket's beginning to leak,' said Fanny. 'If Gudgin doesn't come soon, my ceiling's going to collapse.'

'Perhaps the storm will hurry him up,' muttered Sir George.

'He didn't notice my ceiling the last time he inspected the house,' Fanny grumbled.

'Then you must bang your bedroom door,' suggested Sir George. 'That ought to attract his attention!'

'But it might scare him off altogether,' Fanny replied. 'He's grown uncommon nervous of late.'

Sir George returned to his memoirs. He had reached a favourite episode in his life about the opening of the Suez canal, in November 1856, when he had been aboard the yacht *Deerhound* with a friend of his, Brigadier Bunhaven.

He stopped writing. His memory was beginning to play him tricks. The Brigadier on the yacht hadn't been Bunhaven at all. It had been another Brigadier. Yet, try as he might, Sir George couldn't remember the man's name. At length, exasperated beyond belief, he screwed up what he had written and threw it away.

'I can't remember the wretched fellow's name!' he said irritably as the White Lady appeared and began floating up and down the stairs, because it was Thursday. 'If only I could ask Bunhaven.'

'Perhaps we could get in touch with him!' suggested the White Lady.

'Don't be ridiculous!' snorted Sir George. 'He's been dead longer than I have!'

'Surely you're not going to let a little thing like that deter you!' she replied. 'Why don't we hold a seance?'

'A what?' said Bodkin, appearing suddenly in the fireplace.

'A seance. You know – contact the other side!' explained the White Lady.

'We are the other side,' said Sir George glumly.

'Nonsense! We're only ... er ... halfway.'

'Seances are held by *people*!'

'Not necessarily,' said the White Lady.

She explained that all they needed was a wine glass and the letters of the alphabet. If they put the tips of their fingers on the glass it would glide from letter to letter, spelling out words and answering their questions.

Bodkin didn't like the sound of it. 'We might get in touch with something nasty. Something we couldn't get rid of.'

'It takes about ten minutes to fill,' said Fanny addressing them from the stairs.

'Get a glass, Fanny,' said Sir George.

'That won't do, replied Fanny. 'We need another bucket.'

'We're going to communicate with Bunhaven,' Sir George explained. So while the White Lady chalked the alphabet in a circle on top of a tea-chest, Fanny fetched a wine glass from the Orangery. It was chipped and dusty, but the White Lady didn't think it mattered. She put the glass upside down in the centre of the circle and showed them how they should rest the tips of their fingers on it.

'Now what do we do?' whispered Fanny.

'Make your mind a blank,' replied the White Lady.

'That shouldn't be too difficult,' muttered Bodkin.

'Is there anybody there?' whispered the White Lady.

The door opened and in walked Gudgin wearing a plastic mac and carrying an umbrella.

'He would interrupt,' grunted Sir George.

'Shall I go and bang on the bedroom door?' Fanny asked.

'Good thinking,' said Sir George, 'and keep banging till he comes up.'

Fanny melted away and the others disappeared to the balcony. They watched as Gudgin looked apprehensively at the glass in the alphabet circle.

'That's puzzled him!' said Bodkin.

Upstairs Fanny began banging his bedroom door, and Gudgin jumped in sudden panic.

'Why *is* he so nervous?' asked Sir George.

'It's this house,' said Bodkin. 'It's supposed to be haunted!'

The bedroom door banged and banged, and Gudgin wondered if he'd left an upstairs window open. He was screwing up his courage to go and investigate when Matt appeared by the billiard table, carrying a fishing rod made from a long willow stem. When he saw Gudgin standing indecisively at the bottom of the stairs, a look of wicked glee came over his face. He picked up the umbrella and ran up the stairs.

When Gudgin saw his umbrella floating about he was overwhelmed with icy fear. Matt opened it and drove the terrified man to the door. Then with a final howl, Gudgin scampered away across the terrace.

Matt didn't know he was being watched and collapsed with peals of helpless laughter. But he stopped instantly, when the other ghosts appeared angrily before him.

'How dare you frighten Gudgin like that!' said Sir George.

'What about Fanny's bedroom ceiling?' said Bodkin. 'If you weren't always out gallivanting, you'd know it was letting in the rain.'

By now, the banging upstairs was less insistent.

'That's Fanny, trying to attract Gudgin's attention!' Bodkin angrily explained.

'It may be weeks before he comes back,' said the White Lady.

'If ever,' Bodkin added.

Sir George glared at the boy. 'In the meantime we shall be flooded out!' he said. 'You're a disgrace to Motley!'

Fanny appeared at the top of the stairs.

'Where's Gudgin got to?' he asked plaintively. 'I'm getting awfully tired of banging.'

'Matt scared him off,' said Bodkin.

Fanny looked angrily at Matt. 'You muffin!'

'I shall hold you personally responsible if the roof caves in!' said Sir George indignantly to Matt. 'You're becoming a confounded nuisance. It's high time you began to show ... er ... to show –'

'More respect,' said the White Lady helpfully.

'Yes. More respect,' repeated Sir George. 'Otherwise you'll have to go back to the stables.'

Matt felt the ghosts weren't being very fair. He'd not known about the leak in Fanny's bedroom, and his prank with Gudgin had been quite harmless. He didn't realize that his companions' anger had quite a lot to do with envy. His freedom to come and go as he pleased rankled with them.

Once again the seance got under way and the ghosts sat in a circle with their finger tips touching the wine glass. Bodkin could see that Matt was upset so he made a place for him at the tea-chest. 'We're going to ask it some questions,' he explained.

'Is it a game?' asked Matt.

'Is there anyone there?' the White Lady intoned, shutting her eyes and leaning back with her head turned upward.

'Should there be?' Matt whispered to Bodkin.

'Will you be quiet!' said Sir George, angrily. There was a long silence while the ghosts waited hopefully for something to happen.

'I'm worried about that bucket,' Fanny muttered, as the thunder rolled round Motley Hall and the rain lashed against the windows.

The White Lady addressed the glass again. 'We wish to converse with Brigadier Bunhaven,' she said politely.

'Late of the Twenty-first Lancers –' added Sir George.

Then slowly the glass began to move. It slid across to the letter N and then back to the middle of the circle. After wobbling gently for a moment it skated across to the O. Then it stopped.

'No,' said the ghosts in chorus.

'Who's pushing it?' muttered Sir George, convinced that someone was trying to make a fool of him.

Once again the glass moved. This time it slid to the M then to the A and finally twice to the T.

'Matt!' spelled out the White Lady.

'I ain't pushing it!' said Matt. 'I ain't!'

'Another of your stupid larks!' said Sir George.

The glass began to spin round and round the top of the tea-chest.

'Take your hands off it, you young dog!' roared Sir George.

The moment Matt took his fingers from the glass it stopped gyrating. Sir George snatched it up and brandished it in Matt's face. 'You are a lout and an unmitigated liar!'

'And I'm sick of being yelled at!' Matt shouted back at him.

Sir George was outraged. No one had ever shouted at

him. He put the glass down and stamped over to the fireplace.

'Leave Motley this instant!' he commanded.

In the silence following this outburst, a tiny 'clink' was heard, as a drop of water fell into the wine glass from the ceiling. The ghosts looked up and saw a large crack with beads of water forming along it.

'The bucket's burst!' shouted Fanny, and he vanished swiftly, followed a second later by Sir George and the White Lady.

Drops of water splashed into the glass as Bodkin looked at Matt. 'Are you going?' he asked.

Matt nodded. 'I ain't one of his soldiers to be bullied and shouted at.'

'You were pushing it, weren't you?' said Bodkin.

'No,' replied Matt vehemently. 'I wasn't.'

'Well, something was!'

'It wasn't me!'

Somehow Bodkin knew Matt was telling the truth. 'Let the old cannon-ball cool down and I'll see what I can do,' he promised.

'Why bother?' muttered Matt. 'He won't listen. He never listens.'

'It's all them battles,' Bodkin explained with a smile. 'I think they've left him a bit deaf. Anyhow, it's not the trick you played on Gudgin – or the glass. It goes deeper than that. He envies you, you see.'

Matt was astonished. 'Sir George envies *me*?' he said incredulously.

Bodkin picked up the home-made fishing-rod and smiled wryly. 'We all do,' he said softly. 'Leave it to me. I'll talk him round somehow. Come back in an hour's time.'

Bodkin was just about to vanish when Matt stopped him. 'Who *did* move the glass?' he asked.

Bodkin shrugged. 'I don't know. It's a bit of a mystery, ain't it?'

After Bodkin had disappeared Matt stood for a long time looking at the glass on the tea-chest. If no one had been pushing it, how had it moved? Then, as he stood up, a very curious thing happened. He seemed to leave another Matt behind him, still sitting in the chair. It was as if a person had turned from a mirror and their reflection had stepped out through the glass to follow them. When Matt went to the stables he didn't know that he'd left behind one of the most mischievous of all spirits – a doppelgänger.

A doppelgänger is a kind of spirit twin, and when a ghost brings one of these mysterious creatures into being, albeit unwittingly, they are very hard to get rid of. Doppelgängers are cunning and malicious, and delight in causing upsets and creating quarrels. In fact, the more unhappiness they cause, the stronger they become.

Matt's doppelgänger was no exception. As soon as the real Matt had gone, it picked up the wine glass and shattered it against the fireplace. It laughed wildly and capered round the Great Hall while the lightning flashed and the thunder rumbled outside.

'I'm going to put paid to you for good,' it cackled evilly. 'I'm going to put paid to the lot of you!'

Chapter 12

THE storm was over and Sir George peered through the narrow window of the Bell Tower at the rainbow on the distant horizon. He was already regretting his decision to banish Matt from Motley. In the broken rocking chair the White Lady was reading *Gone with the Wind*.

'D'you think I was a bit hard on the boy?' asked Sir George.

'No, I don't,' replied the White Lady. 'He's been very tiresome and it's time he was punished.'

Sir George was not convinced. 'There's no real harm in him, though, is there?' he muttered. 'And Gudgin's bound to come back anyway.'

The White Lady nodded absently and began reading again.

'Hoppy!' shouted Sir George.

The White Lady dropped her book. 'I beg your pardon?' she said.

Sir George smiled broadly. 'Hopkins!' explained Sir George with a smile of triumph. 'My A.D.C. in Egypt at the opening of the Suez Canal. "Hoppy" Hopkins! Don't you see? That's why I mixed him up with Brigadier Bunhaven. "Hoppy" and "Bunny"!'

Sir George was delighted to have remembered. 'We must continue with my memoirs immediately,' he said. 'It's all coming back to me!'

The White Lady, who had retrieved her book, now

closed it and sat back, prepared to be bored by another of Sir George's interminable reminiscences.

'Dear old "Hoppy" Hopkins! You see, after the procession down the canal, and the banquet and all the speeches, we all went for a ride on dromedaries. Even the Empress Eugenie. It must have been the champagne. Well, Hoppy's beast threw him and hid behind the Sphinx, and he just couldn't catch the wretched animal. And the last I ever saw of poor old Hoppy, he was headin' out across the desert after it, in the general direction of Tripoli . . .'

Sir George's voice trailed away. Then he spoke again more softly. 'I do wish I hadn't told Matt to go,' he said.

'You mustn't weaken, Sir George!' warned the White Lady.

The doppelgänger had been listening intently to all this. Now it slipped quietly into the Bell Tower, looking suitably contrite. 'It's me,' it said humbly.

Sir George and the White Lady were both completely fooled by the doppelgänger's appearance and thought the ghost standing before them really was Matt.

'What do you want?' Sir George asked uncomfortably.

'I want to come back, Sir George,' pleaded the doppelgänger. 'I'm sorry for what I did, moving the glass, and then saying I hadn't. And being disrespectful. Please let me come back to Motley.' And it began sobbing bitterly.

Sir George was disarmed by this unusual display of emotion but the White Lady looked suspicious.

'There, there, old chap,' muttered Sir George, patting the doppelgänger on the back. 'You mustn't be unmanly. As a matter of fact, I've been thinking over my decision and I'm prepared to accept your apology and forget all about it.'

The White Lady sniffed her disapproval at Sir George's change of heart while the doppelgänger went down on one knee and took the General's hand.

'Oh, Sir George! You are too good to me. There's no finer spirit in Motley Hall.' It turned to the White Lady. 'I've always said so – haven't I?' Although Sir George was flattered by this speech the White Lady was disgusted by Matt's apparent grovelling. The doppelgänger noticed her reaction but continued to cringe and fawn round Sir George. 'A real leader,' it said smarmily. 'We're all lucky to serve under you –'

The White Lady couldn't stomach this wheedling hypocrisy a moment longer, and so, with a final contemptuous sniff, she vanished.

The doppelgänger made profit from her sudden departure. 'I often feel that some of us don't appreciate you enough,' it said softly.

This was exactly what Sir George thought, but he said, 'Well, I don't know about that,' and pretended to be embarrassed.

'Bodkin, for instance,' the doppelgänger went on.

'What about Bodkin?' asked Sir George, suddenly very alert.

'He says you aren't fit to be in charge of a hen-coop, let alone Motley Hall,' the doppelgänger lied.

'This is mutiny!' muttered Sir George.

'Ay. That's what he's planning,' whispered the doppelgänger in Sir George's ear. 'He wants to be High Cockalorum himself!'

'Does he indeed!'

'I'd have told you before only it seemed a bit sneaky.'

There was a pause. Sir George wanted to find out more. 'What else has he said?'

'Oh, all kinds of things,' said the doppelgänger smoothly. 'I couldn't repeat some of them. He imitates you sometimes.'

'Imitates me?'

The doppelgänger puffed out its cheeks and strutted up and down, mimicking Sir George. It put its hands behind its back and spoke in pompous tones. 'As I said to the Prince Consort! Gobble-Gobble!'

'Gobble-Gobble?' Sir George repeated.

'He pretends you're a turkey,' said the doppelgänger.

Sir George was outraged. Had Bodkin been there at that moment he would have torn him limb from limb. 'By the thundering guns of Sebastopol!' he roared, striding purposefully towards the stairs.

'No, Sir George, that ain't the way,' said the doppelgänger quickly. 'He'll only deny it. You must catch him in the act!'

Sir George saw the wisdom of this and did his best to simmer down. Then he heard Bodkin come whistling up the steps and his anger began to rise again.

The doppelgänger winked at the General and climbed up to hide behind the old bell just as Bodkin trotted in to plead Matt's case. When Bodkin saw Sir George, however, he thought he looked rather cold and aloof, so he stopped whistling and approached with caution; Sir George had to be handled carefully at the best of times.

'How now, Sir George,' said Bodkin cheerfully. 'The roof's stopped leaking.'

'Has it?' replied Sir George.

Bodkin tried again. 'And all's well.'

'Is it?'

'Isn't it?' asked Bodkin, alarmed to find Sir George looking at him in a most hostile manner. 'Ain't you feeling well?' he asked.

Sir George advanced grimly. 'Never felt better,' he said evenly. 'Never fitter, never brighter, never *sharper*.'

'Oh, that's good,' said Bodkin nervously. 'I'm so pleased.'

'Some of us are born to lead and some to follow,' Sir George went on. 'Ain't that so, Bodkin?'

'Yes,' said Bodkin, by now completely bewildered by Sir George's attitude. 'That's how it usually works.'

'*Then state your business!*' barked the General.

'Eh?'

'Or have you come to study my little idiosyncrasies?'

Bodkin shook his head. 'I've come about Matt . . .'

'Oh, have you?' said Sir George unhelpfully.

'He's not a bad lad, Sir George,' said Bodkin. 'A bit wild sometimes, but very honest. And I thought –'

'You thought, eh?' Sir George interrupted. 'And what did you think?'

'I think we ought to let him come back.'

Sir George put his face very close to Bodkin. '*We* ought to?'

Bodkin realized he'd overstepped the mark and corrected himself. 'Er . . . *you* ought to.'

'So you want to overrule my decision, do you?' said Sir George.

Bodkin was beginning to find the interview very irritating. 'No,' he said, 'I'm just asking you to let him come back.'

'So you can tell the others, you *made* me have him back!'

'Of course not. What do you take me for?'

Sir George's iron control broke. 'I take you for a two-faced malcontent, sir!' he roared.

Bodkin was flabbergasted.

'Gobble-gobble!' said Sir George furiously. 'Gobble-gobble!'

Bodkin didn't like the frenzied gleam in his eyes. Something was very wrong with him.

'I'm a turkey!' snarled the General. '*A turkey!*'

Bodkin tried to get to the door but Sir George cut off his retreat. 'You mutinous dog! The boy's already asked my pardon!' he roared.

'What!' exclaimed Bodkin.

'And I've already granted it. Without any pressure from you!'

Bodkin was even more bewildered. 'Matt came to see you?'

'He did,' replied Sir George coldly.

'Why, the little –' said Bodkin, furious that the boy had made such a fool of him.

'Good day to you, sir,' said Sir George turning on his heel. 'Good day!'

When Bodkin got back to the Great Hall he was full of anger. Matt ran towards him. 'What did Sir George say?' he asked hopefully.

'Make a fool of me, would you?' Bodkin shouted, and gave the boy a tremendous box on the ears.

Matt ducked away, shocked by the sudden attack.

'You tawdry coxcomb! You double-dealing huff-snuff!' Bodkin shouted, and tried to hit him again.

Matt kept dodging Bodkin's blows. 'What's the matter!' gasped Matt, doing his best to avoid the blows raining down on him.

'I'll matter you!' yelled Bodkin. 'You'll smart for it!'

Matt took to his heels and Bodkin chased him all over the house, threatening to beat him soundly when he caught him.

The doppelgänger watched with gleeful triumph.

'I thought you'd been banished!' said a voice and the doppelgänger swung round as Fanny came down the stairs.

'Sir George has pardoned me!' he answered.

Fanny was pleased. He liked Matt and felt Sir George's punishment had been too harsh.

'Have you heard Bodkin's new riddle?' asked the doppelgänger cunningly.

Fanny shook his head. He didn't think Bodkin had any new riddles.

'It's about you!' said the doppelgänger.

Fanny beamed at him unsuspectingly. 'Oh, is it?' he said. 'Then ask me!'

'How many heads has Sir Francis Uproar?'

Fanny thought deeply about this. 'One?' he said at last.

The doppelgänger shook his head. 'No,' it said. 'The answer's four.'

'How so?' Fanny asked, very intrigued.

'Fat-head, thick-head, bone-head and block-head!' said the doppelgänger and ran off before Fanny had a chance to get at it.

The doppelgänger was very pleased with the havoc it was creating, and when it saw the White Lady coming towards it from the Orangery it saw another opportunity to make trouble. It told her that Fanny was looking for her.

The White Lady gave it an unfriendly look. She

hadn't forgotten its nauseating behaviour in the Bell Tower. 'What does he want?' she asked.

'I don't know. But he's very angry.'

'*Fanny* is?' the White Lady said. She couldn't remember Fanny ever being annoyed since he first became a ghost in 1730.

'Ay,' said the doppelgänger. 'He's angry about what you said to Sir George.'

'What I said to Sir George?' repeated the White Lady slowly.

'Ay. About Fanny.'

'I never said anything to him about Fanny!'

The doppelgänger shrugged. 'Well, Sir George told Fanny you did.'

'What exactly am I supposed to have said?'

'That Fanny was an idle good-for-nothing.'

The White Lady looked very indignant. 'I've never said anything of the kind. How dare Sir George make up things like that! Just wait till I see him!'

What fools they all were, thought the doppelgänger. How easy it was to trick them! Soon, with a little help from him, they would all be at each other's throats.

'Fanny's furious,' it went on.

'So he should be,' said the White Lady.

' "Just like the old cat," he said –'

The White Lady's indignation on Fanny's behalf stopped suddenly. 'What did you say?' she said icily.

' "She should have been muzzled long ago",' the doppelgänger concluded.

'Muzzled?' stormed the White Lady. '*Muzzled!* I'll muzzle him, the idle good-for-nothing! Where is he now?'

'In the Great Hall,' said the doppelgänger.

The White Lady tried to vanish but she was in such a state of angry agitation, she couldn't manage it. 'Never mind,' she muttered, 'I'll walk!'

Meanwhile, Bodkin, who was never angry with anyone for long, gave up chasing Matt and returned to the Great Hall where he found Fanny waiting for him.

'Have you seen Matt?' asked Bodkin.

Fanny nodded grimly. 'Oh yes,' he said, 'and he told me your new riddle.'

'What new riddle?'

'Fat-head, thick-head, bone-head, and block-head!' Fanny shouted, accompanying each word with a hard kick. 'You impudent Hawcubite!' he yelled, drawing his sword and belabouring Bodkin with it. 'How many heads have I, you rogue?'

Bodkin jumped out of range, and rubbed himself where it hurt. 'Gloriana!' he exclaimed. 'Another madman!'

'Tell me, you villain!' demanded Fanny, swiping at him again.

'One! One!' Bodkin howled and tried desperately to get away from the stinging blade. It was lucky for him that the White Lady stalked in at this moment and in a voice seething with anger shouted at Fanny to stop behaving like a street-bully.

Fanny lowered his sword, a little scared by her vehemence, only to receive a terrific backhander which sent his wig flying across the room. Then, with her arms flailing like windmills, the White Lady drove him backwards round the billiard table. So bewildered was he by this sudden attack, he did little to defend himself. 'S'death, madam!' he gasped. 'You've knocked my wig off!'

'By heaven, sir, I'll knock your block off!' she cried
'You'd have the old cat muzzled, would you?'

'What old cat?' asked Bodkin, watching the fight
with amazement.

'You keep out of this!' the White Lady stormed.

'I wish I could!' muttered Bodkin.

The situation got even more out of hand, when Sir
George suddenly appeared by the fireplace. The doppel
gänger's words had made the General believe everyone
was against him. 'Still planning to overthrow me?' he
shouted angrily.

'Why did you tell Fanny I said he was an idle good
for-nothing?' the White Lady counter-attacked shrilly

'I never told him anything of the sort!' Sir George
roared back at her.

'You're as mad as May butter – all of you!' cried
Bodkin. 'She thinks she's a cat. You think you're a
turkey. And Fanny don't seem to know how many
heads he's got!'

'None of your gibberish, sir!' snorted Sir George
'None of your Fool's talk, you traitor!'

'I ain't no traitor!' said Bodkin hotly.

They all began hurling accusations and heated de
nials at each other. Nobody really listened and each of
them tried to shout the others down. When this proved
impossible, they stopped shouting and, instead, glared
ferociously at each other, muttering abuse under their
breath.

'You insulted me!' the White Lady told Fanny.

'Who said I did?' said Fanny indignantly.

'Matt!' said the White Lady.

'It was Matt told me your nasty riddle,' said Fanny to
Bodkin.

'What about your imitation of me?' Sir George accused Bodkin.

'What imitation?' asked Bodkin. 'I've never imitated you, Sir George. I swear it. Who told you that I had?'

'Matt,' said Sir George.

The four ghosts realized they'd been tricked into their fighting. 'It seems as if Matt said a lot of things,' said Bodkin quietly.

The doppelgänger, spying from above, gave an evil grin. Everything was working out just as it hoped. After this, the ghosts would never trust Matt again. He would have to spend the rest of eternity by himself.

But Matt had seen the doppelgänger. Hearing the bickering ghosts, he had crept into the Hall to listen. It was a tremendous shock when he saw himself peering down from the gallery; almost like being in two places at once. When his 'twin' waved ironically to him and then disappeared, Matt couldn't bear it any longer and he burst from his hiding place to face the full force of the ghosts' anger.

Sir George commanded him to leave Motley and never return.

Matt was desperate. 'That's just what he wants!' he exclaimed.

'Who wants?' said Bodkin.

'The one that looks just like me!'

'Just like you? One of you is more than enough for us!' Bodkin rejoined sarcastically.

'He was there, I tell you!' Matt insisted, pointing up at the gallery. 'When he saw me he vanished! He's the one that's done all this – not me!'

The White Lady looked searchingly at him. 'Are you trying to say there's a doppelgänger in the house?'

'What's a doppelgänger?' asked Fanny nervously.

'It sounds foreign,' muttered Sir George darkly. 'I don't like the sound of it.'

The White Lady explained. 'It's a spirit double,' she said. 'There's good and bad in everyone. Even ghosts. A doppelgänger is the bad part somehow separated from the good – so that there are two of you.'

'How ridiculous!' exclaimed Sir George.

'No, it's not,' the White Lady said firmly. 'If your doppelgänger does appear he looks exactly like you, down to the last button.'

'Absolute rubbish!' snorted Sir George contemptuously. 'I don't believe it!'

'I didn't believe in ghosts,' said Fanny sadly. 'And look at me now!'

Matt knew that the only way he could clear his name was to find the doppelgänger. The wicked spirit was cunning and would be difficult to trap, so before he set off he gave Bodkin his double-headed penny. 'If I don't ask for it back the next time I see you,' he told him, 'it won't be me. It'll be the ... what you said –'

'Doppelgänger,' the White Lady repeated.

While Matt searched, the ghosts sat round the empty fireplace and pretended there was a fire in the grate. Not that a fire would have warmed them, but they liked to think it would. It made them feel more human.

'What time is it?' asked the White Lady.

Sir George looked at his watch. 'Ten past four,' he muttered.

'It's always ten past four,' she complained peevishly.

Bodkin reminded her in a whisper that Sir George's watch had stopped when he broke his neck in 1896.

'Doppelgängers!' exclaimed Sir George. 'And you

swallowed that story, just as you swallowed all the others!'

'You swallowed them too,' said Bodkin.

'Can I have my penny?' said a voice.

The ghosts didn't know it, but the doppelgänger had been watching when Matt gave Bodkin the penny. It knew that if it claimed it the ghosts would think the real Matt was the doppelgänger. Bodkin handed the penny over and the doppelgänger pocketed it just as Matt ran into the Great Hall.

Bodkin looked at the two Matts standing side by side in front of him. 'Gloriana!' he groaned, 'now what are we going to do?'

'You haven't given him the penny, have you?' Matt asked anxiously.

'Ay, that he has,' grinned the doppelgänger. 'Because I'm Matt.'

'No, you're not! I'm Matt!'

'He must have overheard me,' said the doppelgänger cunningly.

'*He* must have overheard *me*!' said Matt.

'Od's bud,' said Fanny, looking at one Matt and then at the other, like someone at a tennis match, 'I'm cross-eyed looking at 'em.'

'But which one's Matt?' asked the White Lady.

Bodkin looked the two of them up and down and tried to detect the smallest difference. They appeared to be identical. 'Down to the last button,' the White Lady had said . . .

Suddenly Bodkin saw a way to tell them apart. If they were identical then both of them should have a double-headed penny in his pocket! 'If I've given Matt's penny back to him,' said Bodkin slowly, thinking it out, 'they should have one each, but if that one's got two pennies,' – and he pointed at the doppelgänger – 'then he's the doppelgänger.'

Matt held up his arms so that he could be searched. 'I'm Matt,' he said. 'My pockets are empty.'

The doppelgänger cursed them viciously and tried to run off, but Fanny held it while Bodkin searched in its pockets. Then he smiled triumphantly. In his hand were two George III pennies and he turned them over to show the ghosts that both coins were double-headed. 'This one's the doppelgänger all right!'

The wicked spirit glared malevolently at them. It had been outwitted, and all its nastiness boiled over. It shouted curses at them and its face twisted up with malice. Its voice rose to a scream and its shape began to change. It became squat and frog-like, then it shot upwards and became very tall and thin.

While it underwent these extraordinary changes the doppelgänger kept up its torrent of abuse. It began turning green and finally its arms and legs broke off altogether and burst into millions of multi-coloured bubbles. Its head, now hardly recognizable, floated away from its body with yellow and pink steam coming out of the ears. There was a loud bang and the body disappeared altogether. For a moment, the balloon-shaped head glared down at them with huge saucer-like eyes, while a horrible roaring sound came from its grotesque mouth. Then a rumbling sound seemed to shake the whole house and with a final deafening explosion the horrible thing was gone.

'In all my years with Will Shakespeare,' muttered Bodkin during the silence which followed, 'I never had an exit like that!'

Chapter 13

ALTHOUGH Gudgin did his best – and he was a very conscientious man – it was almost impossible to keep people from breaking into Motley. Sometimes boys from the village would dare each other to climb in through one of the ivy-fringed windows; and whenever this happened the spectres scared them away as gently as possible, often by just touching them with their icy fingers, or moaning softly in their ears. Once, two louts broke in and wrote their names on the wall. When Bodkin picked up their bit of chalk and wrote his name as well, they fell over each other in their panic to get out.

Sometimes tramps would use Motley for a day or two, and would even light little fires on the floor to heat up tins of baked beans. This kind of thing was very dangerous, of course, and the ghosts dealt quickly with such thoughtless intruders.

One day, after the ghosts had taken hold of one of these vandals and thrown the terrified man through the back door, they sat round the billiard table discussing the seriousness of the situation.

'In my day,' Sir George told them, 'rascals like that got a seat-full of buckshot if they so much as looked at the gates. Yet now they use the Great Hall as a doss-house.' He shook his head sadly. 'We should never have left India, you know,' he muttered. 'Or anywhere else, come to that . . .'

The White Lady felt that Gudgin was to blame. 'I don't see why we should have to look after Motley for him,' she said.

'He's afraid to come here,' said Bodkin.

'Why are you looking at me,' said the White Lady coldly.

' 'Cos you're the reason!'

Fanny thought that Bodkin was being a little unfair. 'It's not the White Lady's fault Gudgin can see her,' he argued.

'Not her fault?' exclaimed Bodkin. 'Take a look at her!' The ghosts looked at the White Lady, who immediately became very self-conscious and began arranging her dress in aesthetically pleasing folds.

'I mean to say,' Bodkin went on. 'What is she supposed to be? Done up like a mardy May-Queen! Gloriana! – If you could see *anything* – you'd see her.'

'You're not exactly inconspicuous,' snapped the White Lady.

'He's never seen me though, has he?' retorted Bodkin. 'Besides,' – he looked proudly at his clown's smock and pantaloons – 'these are my working clothes. You don't even know why you're dressed like that.'

This was perfectly true but the White Lady wasn't going to admit it. 'Oh, yes I do,' she said. 'It's a . . . It's a bridal gown.'

Bodkin threw back his head and roared with laughter.

'It's not impossible!' she snapped.

'No, just highly unlikely!'

'I'm not staying here to be insulted!'

'Why not? It's as good a place as any!'

After this little exchange the White Lady turned

away from Bodkin and pretended he wasn't there. 'I sometimes wonder if I was a nun,' she said to the others.

'Well, I wouldn't make a *habit* of it,' laughed Bodkin.

'Why is Gudgin so scared?' Matt asked. 'We wouldn't hurt him.'

'We're *different* though, ain't we?' explained Bodkin. 'People get upset by anything they don't understand.'

As well as looking after Motley Hall, Mr Gudgin was also the secretary of a lecture society which met regularly at the local library. He had suggested getting Professor Pogmore from the Institute of Parapsychology to talk to the members. Gudgin had argued that nowadays there was great interest in the supernatural, and Professor Pogmore was a leading figure in this particular field. Gudgin had a personal reason for wanting the Professor to visit their little society, but he kept this to himself.

On the very day the ghosts of Motley Hall had been discussing him, Gudgin drove Professor Pogmore up to the house and led him inside. Pogmore was a tall man with an unruly mop of white hair and a fanatical enthusiasm for his subject. His breezy eccentricity was largely responsible for his great success as a lecturer and TV personality.

'Mainly Elizabethan, I would suppose,' he said, looking round the Great Hall, 'with a few later twiddly-bits.'

The ghosts watched warily from the gallery as Professor Pogmore darted around, examining everything with his piercing eyes.

'I thought as we were passing you might like to see the place,' murmured Gudgin. 'You see, when you agreed to address our little society –'

'You thought – I'll get Pogmore to give Motley Hall the once-over!' cut in the Professor breezily.

Gudgin nodded; this was exactly what he'd thought.

Pogmore sat down, crossed his long legs and clasped his knee in his hands. 'Fire away,' he said cheerfully. 'What exactly have you seen?'

'Do you mean ghosts?' whispered Gudgin after a nervous look round.

Pogmore shook his head impatiently. 'I certainly *don't* mean ghosts. I mean phenomena. There's no such thing as ghosts, my dear chap.'

'The silly great twit!' muttered Bodkin.

Gudgin came nearer to Pogmore. 'In that case, I think I've seen a phenomenon.'

'Where?'

'In the cellars.'

Pogmore pulled an old pipe from his pocket and began to fill it. 'Jolly good,' he murmured. 'Go on.'

'A woman,' breathed Gudgin. 'Dressed in white.'

'Very common,' said Pogmore.

'*Common!*' exclaimed the White Lady indignantly.

'We get a lot of those,' Pogmore went on, stuffing his pipe with tobacco. 'And quite a lot of grey ones too, although they do tend to be mainly monks.' He struck a match and began puffing smoke into the dusty air. 'Did you hear anything?'

'I think she moaned,' Gudgin ventured.

'Not she,' Pogmore corrected. '*It.*'

'*I am not an "It"!*' stormed the White Lady, and vanished to the Bell Tower for a long sulk.

'He's upset her,' said Fanny.

Pogmore went on questioning Gudgin. 'Anything

else? Any footsteps? Any doors opening and closing, or objects floating about?'

'Only my umbrella,' said Gudgin. 'And a sword hilt in the cellar.'

'First-rate!' exclaimed Pogmore. 'I like a bit of telekinesis.'

Gudgin was very relieved to find that Professor Pogmore believed him. Up to now he'd kept his ghostly experiences to himself, and it was a relief to be able to talk about them. Pogmore told him that the Institute of Parapsychology received hundreds of reports all dealing with exactly similar phenomena. There was nothing unusual in Gudgin's experiences.

'What makes me so cross,' said the Professor, 'is the idea of *actual beings* haunting a place year in year out for centuries. It's quite ridiculous.'

This made the ghosts furious. 'Ridiculous?' repeated Sir George, looking angrily at Pogmore.

'You'd have to be a jolly feeble-minded sort of phantom, wouldn't you?' Pogmore continued. 'Hanging around the same place for hundreds of years?'

'This is unsufferable,' cried Sir George, and Fanny and Bodkin were forced to restrain him.

'No,' said Pogmore. 'The idea of ghosts is completely out of date. It just won't wash. Now tell me. How long has Motley Hall been empty?'

'Since the mid fifties,' answered Gudgin.

'First rate! And more or less undisturbed?'

Gudgin nodded.

'Super! That explains everything.'

Pogmore stood up and addressed Gudgin as if he was a large meeting. 'It's all to do with psychically vibrating electro-magnetic wave-patterns. You see, the atmosphere of this place has become charged with these psychically vibrating electro-magnetic wave-patterns, and it is this that has given rise to the various phenomena.'

'Balderdash!' roared Sir George and then he too vanished in a fury.

Pogmore, completely oblivious of the ghosts peering down on him, continued to lecture poor Gudgin. 'Now if you discharge these psychically vibrating electro-wave patterns – Bob's your uncle!'

'Is he?' said Gudgin, who was beginning to get quite out of his depth.

'The phenomena cause visions which are associated not with the so-called supernatural, but with mental processes which take place in the mind of the percipient.' The Professor was striding up and down now, blowing smoke from his pipe like a factory chimney. 'The percipient may have some form of conflict between his conscious and unconscious processes and this causes a degree of disassociation resulting in hallucinatory experiences.'

'What's he talking about?' Matt asked Bodkin.

'Well, it seems to me,' Bodkin replied, 'that according to this camel-faced coxcomb, we ain't ghosts at all, 'cos ghosts are out of date. We're waves and patterns and things.'

'I don't feel like a wave,' said Fanny.

'Neither do I,' said Matt.

'You ain't,' Bodkin reassured them. 'We're ghosts and he's a wind-bag. Come your ways!' And the three of them vanished without another word.

Gudgin looked at Pogmore with a dazed expression. 'How exactly would one discharge the . . .'

'Psychically vibrating electro-magnetic wave-patterns?'

'Yes,' said Gudgin, 'and get rid of the ghosts.'

Pogmore looked pained at the mention of ghosts. 'I am, in fact, working on an experimental piece of equipment designed to disperse exactly the kind of thing you've obviously got here.' The Professor's eyes lit up with scientific zeal. 'I say! I've just had a simply stunning idea! This is the perfect place to test it! I'll cart it over next Saturday!'

So, the following Saturday, Professor Pogmore arrived at Motley with his new invention. It stood on a tripod and looked as if he had managed to cross a trombone with an old-fashioned machine-gun. The Professor's colleagues at the Institute of Parapsychology had christened the thing Pogmore's De-Spooker, or the P.D.S. for short.

'It's based on a modified type of oscillator,' he explained, his white hair looking even wilder than usual, 'wired up to various bits and bobs, amplifiers and various electronics still in the experimental stage.'

After he had plugged the odd-looking components together, the Professor took an empty milk bottle and stood it on the billiard table. 'I'll show you how the jolly old thing works,' he said cheerfully.

Gudgin, who was beginning to wonder why he had ever thought of bringing the Professor to Motley Hall in the first place, put on his glasses.

'It's only a prototype of course,' muttered Pogmore, adjusting the outrageous-looking contraption, 'and it's not nearly as portable as I'd like. I'm afraid I haven't got all the bugs out yet.'

He switched on and his invention emitted a rude burp. 'Oh dear,' he said, 'it shouldn't do that.'

Matt had watched him arrive and was sitting on the stairs, trying to puzzle out what he was up to.

'When did they get here?' asked Fanny, suddenly appearing beside him.

'An hour ago,' replied Matt. 'And the thin fellow's not said one word I can understand!'

A rich humming note filled the air and the Professor turned Pogmore's De-Spooker to point directly at the milk bottle. The sound grew louder as he carefully adjusted various knobs. At the same time the note rose steadily in pitch until Gudgin had to put his hands over his ears. Remorselessly the sound climbed higher and higher until it was almost unbearable. The milk bottle rocked on its base and began to vibrate. Finally when the P.D.S. was screaming like a soul in torment the glass shattered.

But that wasn't the only thing that had happened, for Mr Gudgin was ruefully looking at his ruined glasses, which had just as suddenly frosted over with hundreds of cracks. Professor Pogmore, nothing daunted, muttered something about sending the bill to him, and went straight back to fiddling with his invention.

'It really shows you what sound-waves can do, doesn't it?' he said. 'Now if my theory is correct, and I'm pretty sure it is, ultra-sonic sounds, so high we can't hear them, will wipe out your so-called ghosts for good!'

'S'death! The villain means it!' Fanny exclaimed, and vanished to warn the others.

Gudgin was beginning to have a twinge of conscience about de-spooking Motley Hall. It was all very well for the Professor to talk about psychically vibrating thingummies, but Gudgin had seen the White Lady, and she looked like a ghost to him. Although the fact that the house was haunted was making it difficult to sell, the ghosts hadn't actually done anyone any harm. Professor Pogmore, on the other hand, seemed to think that eliminating ghosts wasn't any different from wiping out death-watch bettle.

While Gudgin was having second thoughts about the De-Spooker, Sir George and the White Lady were playing snakes and ladders in the Bell Tower. The White Lady didn't like playing with Sir George because he became emotionally involved and hated losing. He always cheated and she always let him, though sometimes it was impossible for her *not* to win. When this happened Sir George would get very hurt and sit silently by himself for hours afterwards, looking at the wall.

He had just landed on a snake when Fanny and Matt appeared in the Bell Tower and told him about Pogmore's De-Spooker.

'He's brought a screaming post-horn to destroy us!' said Fanny.

'Calm yourself, Francis,' muttered Sir George, surreptitiously pushing his counter forward a few squares, 'you're overwrought. We can't be destroyed by a post-horn.'

'What about the walls of Jericho!' said Fanny.

'That was trumpets,' said Sir George firmly. 'Not post-horns.'

The White Lady rattled the dice, threw a six, and landed at the bottom of the longest ladder. As Sir George hadn't noticed, she pushed it forward to a snake.

'You didn't see how this thing smashed the glass!' said Matt.

'Ghosts and glass are made of very different substances,' said Sir George pompously.

'It's no use putting your head in the sand, Sir George,' said Fanny. 'He's out to get rid of us for good.'

Sir George rattled the dice, threw a one, and glared up at Fanny as if it was his fault. 'Alarmist chatter! The beggar will play with his silly contraption until he's bored with it, and then he'll leave us in peace.'

'I think you should come, Sir George,' said Matt.

Sir George shook his head. 'I've better things to do,' he said, waiting for the White Lady to throw the dice.

It was obvious that snakes and ladders meant more to Sir George than his own survival, so Fanny and Matt looked for Bodkin. Perhaps he would realize the seriousness of the situation.

Pogmore, in the meantime, had switched on the De-Spooker again. The screaming noise was deafening, and a few pieces of plaster fell from the ceiling. The professor threw another switch and the sound climbed beyond the range of the human ear. Even the De-Spooker began to tremble.

At this moment Bodkin capered into the Great Hall playing his recorder. When he saw Gudgin and Pogmore he stopped dancing and went to have a closer look at the P.D.S. Was it a new musical instrument?

'Move the thing round a bit, would you?' Pogmore asked Gudgin.

'I'd really rather you did it,' Gudgin replied nervously.

'Nonsense!' said Pogmore. 'It won't bite!'

Gudgin approached the machine gingerly and swivelled it round until it was pointing straight at Bodkin. The sound waves rippled through him and he began fading away. Despite a tremendous effort to stay looking solid, he rapidly became transparent. He felt sick and dizzy. At the same time he was overcome with a sense of the most profound melancholy. 'Gloriana!' he whispered anxiously. 'What's happening to me?'

In a state of wild panic Bodkin rushed up to the Bell Tower, where Sir George, who had won the game of snakes and ladders, stared curiously at him. 'I say, Bodkin,' he said, 'you look a bit peaky.'

'Peaky. *Peaky! I'm fading away!*'

'Don't be absurd,' said the White Lady, pushing the board to one side. 'You're just a little off-colour, that's all.'

Bodkin pointed at himself with despair. 'Look at me!' he howled. He was standing with the bell rope hanging down behind him and it could be seen quite clearly through his chest.

'Nothing to worry about, old chap,' grunted Sir George. 'It's probably something to do with local atmospheric conditions. The prevailing wind. A deep depression over ... er ... somewhere or other.'

'Deep depression?' cried Bodkin. '*I'm melting!*'

'Fiddlesticks!' Sir George replied.

'I'm a shadow of my former self,' Bodkin went on desperately. 'And that wasn't exactly solid! It's that maniac in the Great Hall who's done this to me!'

'He walked right into it!' said Fanny, appearing suddenly with Matt at his side.

'I don't want to go to limbo,' Bodkin whimpered.

'Where's that?' asked Matt.

'Nowhere,' said Fanny.

'Don't you see?' Bodkin lamented, 'I'm dissolving! Don't you understand? I'm leaving Motley for ever! I haven't been much for the last four hundred years, but I'll be nothing at all from now on!'

The ghosts urged him not to give way to despair and, if possible, to pull himself together.

'I feel faint,' said Bodkin.

'You are,' agreed the White Lady. 'Very faint.'

'And getting fainter,' added Matt anxiously.

'Perhaps a glass of brandy –?' suggested Sir George sympathetically.

'I never touch spirits,' said Bodkin, who despite his faded condition couldn't resist a pun. Then he began to flicker in the most alarming manner until there was hardly anything left of him at all. His companions crowded round and helped him into the rocking-chair.

'I'm going!' he gasped and disappeared completely. Then after a moment, a faint blur, barely recognizable as Bodkin, reappeared in the rocking-chair.

'Goodbye, Sir George,' he whispered, and held out a shadowy hand.

Sir George was in tears. 'My dear old friend,' he said brokenly.

The pale phantom tried hard to smile. 'Farewell, Fanny,' he said. 'Forgive all my rude remarks, White Lady. I didn't really mean them, you know ...' Again Bodkin melted mysteriously away.

'Don't go yet, Bodders!' Fanny pleaded, tears running down his face.

Just for a moment, the faintest flicker of what had once been Bodkin returned to the chair. 'Did I ever tell you the joke about ...?' Then he had gone; and the ghosts stood silent. Fanny took off his wig and bent his head so that the others wouldn't see his tears. But they were crying too. Bodkin had been the most cheerful ghost of them all. He had always tried to make them laugh whenever they'd been unhappy, and although he had often teased them, he'd never said anything really mean or hurtful.

'I shall never forgive Gudgin for this, as long as I li – stay here,' swore Sir George.

'And if he has his way,' Matt warned them grimly, 'that ain't going to be very long!'

Chapter 14

In the Great Hall, Professor Pogmore and Mr Gudgin stood and watched the P.D.S. vibrating gently on its stand. Red needles swung to and fro on the dials, and various bits of the equipment hummed and whined. The De-Spooker was now operating far beyond the range of human hearing.

Professor Pogmore wrote busily in his notebook for several minutes while Gudgin stood uneasily beside him and wondered what was going to happen next. The Professor checked his notes quickly and switched off his invention, which became ear-splittingly audible before howling down to its lowest note and cutting out altogether. It reminded Gudgin of a jet engine being switched off.

Professor Pogmore ran his bony fingers through his hair and sighed with satisfaction. 'I doubt if any psychically vibrating electro-magnetic wave-patterns are left in here now. We've given the room a three-hundred-and-sixty-degree sweep.' He bit hungrily into a huge cheese roll and scattered crumbs all over the billiard table.

'We shan't know for certain of course,' he mumbled, chewing vigorously. 'However, unless you send us a report indicating the continued presence of psychic phenomena, I'll be pretty sure I'm on the right track with ultra-sonics.'

Meanwhile a grim council of war was being held in

the Bell Tower. It was chaired by Sir George who was now fanatically determined to avenge the disappearance of his friend. The situation was very grave, he told them. The cowardly and unprovoked attack had been mounted without warning and had taken them completely by surprise.

'The infernal machine is obviously lethal,' Sir George warned them. 'If we allow this power-mad despot to complete his plan, then there is no doubt in my mind that we shall all suffer the same fate as our sadly-missed colleague. A fate best described as – *electrical exorcism!*' He paused to let the full horror of his words sink in. 'Now, as a professional soldier, I know that any head-on attack against the enemy possessing a weapon of such undoubted superiority would be a rash and foolish venture –'

'Od's bud, Sir George!' cried Fanny leaping to his feet, eager to do something dreadful to Professor Pogmore.

'Sit down, sir!' ordered Sir George tersely. 'We cannot afford any more casualties. As a student of Clausewitz –'

'Who's he?' asked Matt.

'– as a student, I say, of Clausewitz,' Sir George ploughed on, 'I see no point in being wiped out through unnecessary heroics.'

Fanny, who was feeling particularly heroic at the moment, muttered 'Shame!' and glared at Sir George, who pretended not to notice.

'We shall remain calm,' he said.

This time Fanny could bear it no longer. He drew his sword and waved it in the air. 'Up the Uproars!' he yelled defiantly.

'If you continue this irrational display, Fanny,' Sir George threatened, 'I'll have you court-martialled for insubordination.'

'A fig for your court-martial,' answered Fanny. 'I'm going down to the Great Hall to slaughter them both!'

The White Lady reminded him gently that his slaughtering days had been over since 1730 and managed to calm him down.

'By heavens!' muttered Fanny. 'If I had any blood, it would be *boiling*!'

'The real villain is that treacherous renegade Gudgin,' said Sir George.

The White Lady nodded. 'I never liked him. It's his ears. But all the same, I'm the only one that can talk to him, and that's what I'm going to do.'

Sir George and the others welcomed this plan enthusiastically. Perhaps if she could impress on Gudgin the dire results of the Professor's interference, he might well ask the man to leave.

In the Great Hall, while Pogmore finished his tea-break, Gudgin showed him a plan of the house, in the old Guide Book. Pogmore looked interested. 'Any particularly eerie spots?' he asked.

'The Bell Tower is supposed to be haunted,' Gudgin replied.

'First rate! Towers are absolutely top-hole places for storing psychokinetic energy. Heaven knows why.'

'The bell used to toll by itself,' Gudgin told him. 'Especially after a death in the family.'

'Clever old bell,' laughed Pogmore. 'Just another example of gestalt mood actually generating telekinesis.' He looked dubiously at the P.D.S. 'I hope we've got enough cable to reach the Bell Tower. Perhaps we ought to do the cellars first.' He lifted the horn of the P.D.S. from its pedestal and handed it to Gudgin.

However, Gudgin had no intention of going down into the cellars, even armed with the P.D.S. 'I'd really rather not,' he remonstrated, 'I might see something.'

'I hope you will, old boy,' Pogmore replied. 'In fact – I'm relying on it.'

'But I suffer from claustrophobia,' Gudgin insisted desperately. 'Please, Professor Pogmore, don't make me go down into the cellars!'

Pogmore realized Gudgin was very frightened, so he took the De-Spooker from him. He had no fear of phenomena. 'I won't hallucinate though,' he said gloomily, 'I never see *anything*.

'Mind you,' he called cheerfully as he began going down into the cellars, 'I haven't had such fun since I wired up my rubber plant to a lie-detector.'

Gudgin breathed a sigh of relief and sat down by the controls of the P.D.S. and tried to remember how the Professor had switched it on. He was so busy puzzling it out, he didn't notice the White Lady glide up to him. She touched him gently to attract his attention, and Gudgin held his breath. Then slowly he turned his head until, out of the corner of his eye, he could see a pale hand resting on his shoulder. 'Gudgin,' the White Lady whispered softly in his ear, 'I must talk to you!'

Gudgin's nerve snapped. He leapt up, knocking over his chair, and ran blindly from the 'thing' behind him. But the White Lady was not to be thwarted, and chased after him, her long sleeves floating out like the wings of some unearthly bird. Down the dark passages fled Gudgin, his mouth dry as dust, his heart pounding. Whenever he looked back, the white figure was still there. At last he skidded into the kitchen and tried to hide in the pantry. But he was in such a panic he couldn't get the door open, so he had to turn and face the ghastly apparition. 'What do you want? Why are you haunting me?' he cried hoarsely.

'If you stop running away all the time, I'll tell you!' said the White Lady.

'Oh leave me alone – please leave me alone!'

'When we've had our little chat.'

'But I don't want a little chat,' Gudgin whispered. 'We've absolutely nothing in common!'

'Oh, but we have! We've something very important in common. Don't you want to know what it is?'

Gudgin frantically shook his head and pressed himself back against the pantry door.

'Electrical exorcism!' hissed the White Lady.

Meanwhile Professor Pogmore had been calling from the cellars for Gudgin to switch on the De-Spooker. When there was no response he stamped angrily up to the Great Hall again. Gudgin was nowhere to be seen. 'Where's he got to?' he muttered impatiently. Behind him, glaring fiercely at the De-Spooker, was Sir George Uproar.

Sir George had come down from the Bell Tower to see if the White Lady had managed to contact Gudgin. Intrigued by all the electronic equipment on the billiard table, he had approached for a closer look, and it was then that Pogmore saw him. 'Who on earth are you?' he asked. He had never seen a ghost before, and, what's more, he didn't believe in them. As far as he was concerned the old boy was simply a stranger.

Sir George decided to brazen it out by pretending to

be human. 'I'm a friend of Gudgin's,' he said airily.
... er ... heard he was in here today so I ... popped
round.'

'He didn't say anything about anyone else coming!'
said Professor Pogmore, puzzled by the General's old-
fashioned appearance.

'Oh ... didn't he?' Sir George replied uneasily. 'Well,
well.'

'I'm Pogmore,' said the Professor, holding out his
hand.

'And I'm Uproar,' said Sir George, putting his behind
his back. Too late he realized the mistake he'd made in
mentioning his name. Gudgin must surely have told
Pogmore that the Uproar family was no more.

Pogmore, still rather puzzled, looked past Sir George
at the picture over the fireplace, And recognized who it
was!

'Jumping Jehosophat!' he exclaimed. 'You're a pro-
jection from my subconscious!'

Sir George was furious. He wasn't anything of the
sort. 'You insolent beggar!' he exclaimed.

'It's the painting!' murmured Pogmore to himself.
'Somehow I'm projecting the painting!'

'That, sir, is my portrait!' said Sir George, trembling
with suppressed fury.

'You are the very first hallucination I've ever had!'
remarked Pogmore, completely unruffled. And he took
his own pulse and timed it with his watch.

Sir George was quite put out. He had never been
described as an hallucination before – at least, not to his
face. Obviously it was meant to be an insult. 'You are a
mushroom, sir! An upstart!'

re shook his head calmly. 'Strictly speaking,
_ the upstart, because I exist and you don't. You
_erely an illusion in my brain.'

_reat Gladstone,' bellowed Sir George. 'I am the
spirit of Sir George Uproar!'

But again Pogmore shook his head. 'No. You are a
psychically vibrating electro-magnetic wave-pattern!'

'I know what I am!' roared Sir George truculently.

'You don't know anything of the sort,' replied Pogmore complacently. 'You haven't got a mind, you see.
At least, not one of your own. You're part of mine!'

'You confounded schoolmaster! I lived in this house!
I am Sir George Uproar!'

'You can't be,' said Pogmore craftily. 'Sir George
Uproar is dead.'

'Don't be clever with me –'

'So, don't you see, I'm really talking to myself.'

Sir George had never been so slighted. 'I shall go mad
in a minute!' he gasped.

'No, you won't,' the Professor answered with a self-
satisfied smile. 'I shan't let you!'

'Pack up this dreadful contraption of yours and get
out!' roared Sir George. 'You've done enough damage
already!'

Pogmore's answer to this was quite simple. He turned
the P.D.S. to face him and switched it on. The ultra-
sonic waves hit Sir George head-on and he immediately
began to disintegrate. Horror-stricken, the old General
looked at his arm and saw that it was already transparent. 'You can't do this to me!' he gasped.

'I'm doing it!' the Professor replied. 'Now we'll see
who's real and who isn't, won't we?'

Sir George had been in some tight corners during his

military career but never anything like this. 'Fanny!' he called at the top of his voice.

'Look at you – you old mirage!' jeered Pogmore. 'That painting up there is more real than you are!'

Sir George made a desperate effort to grab his tormentor, but the relentless power of the P.D.S. drove him back.

'The last battle! No surrender! Up the Uproars!' cried the fading image of Sir George. Then, accepting that the end had finally come, he stood to attention, saluted, and faded away as all old soldiers should.

Professor Pogmore was well pleased with himself and highly delighted with his invention. 'Spectacular!' he muttered, patting the P.D.S. 'It works! It really works! Total eclipse of stout party!' He had to tell Gudgin his news, but where was the wretched little man? Leaving the P.D.S. throbbing away at full blast he ran off in search of him.

With his back still pressed against the pantry door, Gudgin was still being interrogated by the White Lady. 'I can't sell Motley,' Gudgin explained desperately, 'because you've given it such a bad reputation!'

The White Lady bridled indignantly. 'How dare you!'

'Oh, I don't mean you personally. I know it was wrong of me but I thought that if I . . . if someone . . . if there were no ghosts . . . I might be able to sell it.'

'So you were driven by greed,' said the White Lady.

'No, no! *Concern!* I want to see Motley come to life again. I'm sorry, I seem to be saying all the wrong things. When Professor Pogmore came down, well, it seemed such a golden opportunity to – to – change things.'

At this moment the Professor strode into the kitchen. He couldn't see the White Lady of course, and was surprised to find Gudgin cowering against the pantry with a terror-stricken expression on his face. 'My dear chap,' he said excitedly. 'I've been looking everywhere for you –'

'She's there!' whispered Gudgin, pointing at the White Lady.

'Is she?' Pogmore exclaimed. 'First rate!'

'Can't you see her?' gasped Gudgin.

'Don't be silly,' the Professor replied. 'She's in your subconscious, not mine. You'd hardly credit it, but I just dreamed up the old buffer in that painting over the fireplace! I wish you'd been there – except of course you wouldn't have seen him.' Pogmore corrected himself – 'I mean "it", of course ... It was great fun. I lined up the old De-Spooker and wiped him off the ether! Most spectacular – it really was!'

The White Lady gave a heart-rending wail of concern and rushed back to the Great Hall.

'Listen to me, Pogmore,' said Gudgin desperately, 'you're wrong! They're not projections! They're not vibrating waves! They are *ghosts*! And if there are any left in Motley, they'll never forgive me!'

Matt and Fanny meanwhile had waited anxiously for news. When neither of their companions came back to the Bell Tower they became very apprehensive. Had both Sir George and the White Lady been wiped out by Pogmore's De-Spooker? They crept cautiously down to the Great Hall to find out.

Matt could see that the dreadful machine was still on, and he warned Fanny not to walk in front of it.

'Sir George is no more!' howled the White Lady, rushing across to them in despair.

'Look out!' Fanny shouted, and tried to push her out of the way.

It was too late. The full force of the sonic beam caught them both and they began fading away almost at once.

The White Lady looked into Fanny's eyes. 'You tried to save me!' she said softly.

Fanny smiled bravely. 'I always was an impetuous idiot,' he whispered. 'Not very bright – but very impetuous.'

'So this is the end.'

'Absolutely.'

'Am I very faint?' asked the White Lady, who had always been worried about her appearance.

'Yes,' said Fanny. 'Am I?'

The White Lady nodded and then drew very close to him. 'I'll let you into a little secret,' she said softly.

'Yes?'

But whatever the secret was, there was no time left for either of them. With the merest whisper of a sigh, they vanished.

Matt had never felt so lonely before. The long years of haunting the stables had been nothing to this. Since coming into Motley, his existence had completely changed. The other ghosts had become his close friends and he'd learnt all sorts of interesting and unusual things from them. Now they were gone, never to return.

He was so distressed that he hardly noticed when Professor Pogmore began gloomily packing up his mass of electronic equipment, persuaded at last to stop his experiments.

The Professor had no wish to upset Gudgin. If the little chap wanted to believe that psychic phenomena were actual beings, with their own minds and feelings, then who was he to tell him any different? Gudgin was wrong of course, but the world would always be full of ignorant, superstitious people who believed in old-fashioned things like ghosts.

Darkness fell, but Matt still couldn't bear to leave Motley and go back to the stables. He stood in the moonlight and looked up at the picture of Sir George.

He remembered how Brayling and Penrose had plotted to pull down the old house and how Bodkin had tricked them in the end. He remembered the famous fight with Bad Lord William. He remembered the havoc his doppelgänger had caused.

Sir George's portrait stared down at him. How funny it had looked when he had drawn those sooty spectacles on it! All the fun and excitement was over now.

'What does it feel like to be nothing at all?' he whispered sadly.

'Like a joke you've forgotten,' a familiar voice answered.

It was Bodkin! He was standing behind Matt with the other ghosts.

'But I thought –' Matt stammered.

Bodkin shook his head. 'Pogmore's got a lot of work to do on that machine of his before it drops a final curtain on the ghosts of Motley!'

'The infernal machine was devastating,' summed up Sir George, 'but by no means final.'

Matt gave a great whoop of delight, and the next

moment everybody was laughing and patting him on the back.

'We have won through, my friends!' boomed Sir George above all the excitement. 'The day is ours!'

'We must celebrate!' cried Fanny.

'A song!' suggested the White Lady.

'What about the "Motley Round"?' said Bodkin, who had written it. Sir George thought this was a splendid idea but insisted on beginning, so Bodkin hummed the note for him. Then he had to hum the whole thing because Sir George had forgotten the tune.

Thus the ghosts celebrated their survival with Sir George singing the first line of the round and the rest of them chiming in, one after the other. They sang it again and again, until the words echoed and re-echoed through the creaking house and the cobwebs shook.

'Sing we all of Motley Hall
Motley Hall! Motley Hall!
Home for us whatever may befall.
Ding dong! Ghosts all!'

If you have enjoyed reading this book and would like to know about others which we publish, why not join the Puffin Club? You will be sent the club magazine, *Puffin Post*, four times a year and a smart badge and membership book. You will also be able to enter all the competitions. For details of cost and an application form, send a stamped addressed envelope to:

The Puffin Club Dept A
Penguin Books Limited
Bath Road
Harmondsworth
Middlesex

and if you live in Australia, please write to:

The Australian Puffin Club
Penguin Books Australia Limited
P.O. Box 257
Ringwood
Victoria 3134